WOLF'S
Passion

ELIZABETH LAPTHORNE

ELLORA'S CAVE
ROMANTICA PUBLISHING

What the critics are saying...

ဢ

5/5 stars "Ice (and plenty of it) is needed while you read this book. *Ms Lapthorne* continues the story of the Rutledge brothers in *The Mating Game*. Ms. *Lapthorne* truly draws pictures with her words and I raced through this book. I can't wait for the next installment in this series, which put such a smile in my heart." ~ *Just Erotic Romance Reviews*

5/5 Unicorns "Hot, Hot, Hot! *The Mating Game* by *Elizabeth Lapthorne* is full of erotic love scenes. The reader easily pictures the excitement that Dom feels for the hunt and it is fun to watch him go after Mary. I loved the other two books, and would recommend to all paranormal readers this series. However, Dominic's story is my favorite." ~ *Enchanted in Romance*

4.5/5 hearts "*Ms. Lapthorne* has done it again! Her Rutledge Wolves Series is at its finest here; with the telling of Dominic's search for his mate [...] Her multidimensional characters are filled with many sensual delights and emotional lures that will captivate the reader from the beginning. Kudos to *Ms. Lapthorne* in creating a superb family filled with many dynamics and full of hot wild passion" ~ *Love Romances*

"Once again, *Ms. Lapthorne* has scored a hit with this book. Samuel and Chloe are fully developed characters that will draw readers into their story [...] The sexual escapades between them are entertaining as well as arousing. The author does a great job of blending it within the plot, as it doesn't seem to be out of place or overdone." ~ *Fallen Angels Reviews*

An Ellora's Cave Romantica Publication

www.ellorascave.com

Also by Elizabeth Lapthorne

෨

About the Author

&

Elizabeth Lapthorne has been writing professionally since 2002. She has been astonished by the sucess of her Rutledge Werewolf series, and finds immense pleasure in hearing from her fans. To date she has more than ten books out, a few of those even in paperback.

Elizabeth regularly goes to the gym to chew over her ideas; many a book has begun or been worked through while cycling on the bikes. She also loves to read, eat chocolate and talk for hours with her friends. Elizabeth would love to hear from her fans, and checks her email religiously.

Elizabeth welcomes comments from readers. You can find her website and email address on her author bio page at www.ellorascave.com.

Tell Us What You Think

We appreciate hearing reader opinions about our books. You can email us at Comments@EllorasCave.com.

WOLF'S PASSION

ഔ

THE MATING GAME
~13~

MY HEART'S PASSION
~125~

THE MATING GAME

അ

Dedication

For my very own Mar, who loved Dom first
Liz

Chapter One

୫

From: samuel@rutledgesecurity.com

To:artemais@rutledgesecurity.com;william@rutledgesecurity.com; dominic@rutledgesecurity.com

Subject: Our brother—the budding writer!

Attach: (Untitled doc.)

Hey there, brothers mine.

Seems the youngest of us is trying to become a budding writer. I found this, left ever-so-stupidly, on an unsecured part of the computer while I was doing the routine security check on the work files.

See you tonight, wolf boy. Can't wait to start ribbing you about this. Just had to share with our loving family.

Samuel

<Attachment included>

I feel her pull on me as She shines on my face through the open curtains. Even though it's the night before She is Full, She retains this immense hold over me. After all these years, I still can't figure out if Her hold on me is good or bad. She calls to me no matter how hard I try to hide. When I finally give in to Her embrace I receive indescribable joy, passion, and freedom. I wonder again why I resist her call. Is it simply my desire to rule my own destiny? Or do I fight Her so hard each month simply from my own stubbornness? If so, then why would I always give in as She rises at dusk, full and rounded and far more beautiful than any woman I have ever come across?

Maybe my melancholy is from my weariness of the constant fucking. Seeing Artemais and William so sickeningly happy makes me wonder if there is more to women than simply bedding and shedding them the next morning. Yet the few times I tried forging deeper relationships they ended with female tears and recriminations. It makes one wonder what really does go on in the female mind.

The Mistress of the Moon I can understand. One night a month She compels my siblings and I, along with our pack, for her devotion, to worship her. Merely sitting here and thinking of the freedom, the scents, the hunt, and wild runs in the forest is enough to make my meat stand up at attention. While I might fuck in my other form occasionally, this boner isn't a sexual one, it's more standing to attention in respect for the One whom I must follow, the One whom I can't resist. Why can't I meet a woman like that? One I truly can't resist.

Goddess knows I enjoy women. I love their hair, their scent, a million small things about them from their taste to their texture. Yet when I look at my mated brothers, have I ever truly felt that level of devotion, of adoration to anyone except the moon? It must be thoughts like this that make me wake restless and frustrated next to forgettable women each and every night. The eternal question, "Would I be upset if I never saw this woman again?" rocks around my head.

Both Art and Wills have told me separately that they would die a million deaths if anything happened to their mates. The fact I can wallow and momentarily forget my frustration in my casual women doesn't answer the fact that they are all the same to me. All forgettable.

I care about them; I care that they reach their pleasure and enjoy their short time with me. But there have been so very many that they blur, much like those few seconds when I change from man to wolf.

I'm waiting for the punch line — when I wake up one morning beside a woman I realize I couldn't possibly leave or let go of. Much like, resist as I do the desirable, full moon, I feel a constant ache in my heart when She finally falls beyond the horizon and dawn breaks, and I am once again left alone, to my endless fucking and searching.

Tending to my rampant cock alone merely exasperates this loneliness, this frustration. As I pump myself to a heady release, the loss and frustration levels inside me mount.

I can tell it is the night before the full moon because I feel so melancholy tonight. My desire, even after spending three hours with the lusty brunette in my bed, Shawna I think her name is...even now, minutes after the attention of my own hand, my rampant cock is aroused again merely from the thoughts of tomorrow night, when I can run wild and free. Maybe I should go back to Shawna and —

Mary snapped back to attention. She turned quickly to double-check her young cousin, Matthew, still paced on the other side of the room by the large window, and wasn't reading the incredibly sexy, erotic, private thoughts she had stumbled onto over her shoulder.

Noting her attention on him, he halted a moment. "Have you untangled me yet?"

Typing a few quick keystrokes, Mary closed the email she had accidentally opened. Thinking it one of the portal exits she was searching for, she had at first been surprised to realize it was a saved email. Initially confused, she had quickly begun to scan the email. The depth of feeling in the email's words, the true and uncensored thoughts of the man who had written them had instantly snared her attention, capturing her as securely as her young cousin had been caught in the tricky trap laid out by the Security Company.

Thankfully, before she invaded Dominic Rutledge's privacy too much, she had been recalled to her surroundings. She was not in some decadent bedroom, listening to that man whisper his secrets in her ear. She was here in her home office, trying to untangle her wretched cousin from his idiocy.

"Nearly. What the hell were you doing, hacking into a *security* company of all things, Matthew? *Honestly.* How many times do I have to tell you this isn't some stupid game with no repercussions?"

Mary returned her attention back to the computer.

Despite the hot feeling thrumming through her body, she forced her mind back to the task at hand. She must extract her eighteen-year-old cousin from the quagmire he'd created.

Matthew resumed his restless pacing, and Mary entered a few more keystrokes, silently cursing her overenthusiastic cousin. The virus scan finished ten minutes later and she switched off the computer. She leaned back in her chair with a sigh.

"I swear, next time you use my computer, it had better be for those blasted killing games of yours, not this dumb hacker joke your friends keep on goading you into. It won't be *them* sitting in the jail cell I'll have to bail out." She held up her hand as Matthew opened his mouth to protest.

"And no, the nice police officers aren't going to care for the excuse 'But they dared me!' Matthew, you're eighteen. I know you kick ass in the computer industry, but frankly a jail record will kill any hopes you have for *ever* getting a decent job."

Matthew scuffed one foot into her carpet, much like he had when caught stealing cookies from the jar when he was eight.

"I'm sorry, Mary. I'll try not to let them goad me again. I proved I wasn't good enough to get out. I could tell they were tracking me, though. Show me how you got us out."

"What's this 'us' business, buddy? You got yourself in; you can learn next time to get yourself out." At Matthew's pleading look, Mary relented.

Matthew and his older sister, Chloe, might technically be her cousins, but they were as close as siblings. Having been raised together, even annoyed as she was at Matthew's delve into hacking, she knew she would eventually show him how she escaped the fierce clutches of the Rutledge Security Company. Flashing his most charming grin, Matthew sent her a cheerfully pleading look.

"Later, buddy. But no more hacking. You want to test out

your skills, you wait for your college course to start, or better yet, get a *job*."

"Tonight, then?" At Mary's raised eyebrow Matthew grumbled his assent. "Oh, all right. Thanks again."

Mary returned his kiss on the cheek, and sat back in her chair as Matthew left her small home office. She thought back to the email she'd discovered accidentally.

Surely it was some sort of joke? It had to be some idiotic male prank? Switching her computer back on, she logged on the Internet and did a quick search.

Well shit, there really is a Rutledge Security company! And in Montana of all places!

She lived on the border between Montana and North Dakota. From the look of things, Rutledge Security was situated up the northwest corner of Montana.

Mary searched a little deeper, and found the founders of the company were a group of four brothers. Artemais, William, Samuel, and Dominic Rutledge. *Not good, not good at all for my peace of mind.*

It seemed as if Artemais, the eldest, pretty much ran the company, with a bit of help from his brothers. The picture under the "About Us" link showed four drop-dead gorgeous men. The men shown as Artemais and William appeared happily married with a number of kids between them. There were a lot of happy family snaps showing the beaming men with strong arms wrapped around very satisfied looking women.

Other photos showed the same men and women with happy, healthy-looking kids. Samuel and Dominic, while shown playing with the kids, still cheekily winked out from the pictures, obviously single.

Surely if they were werewolves they couldn't be happily married? Mary thought back to Dominic's comments about Art and Wills being "happily mated" and "dying a thousand deaths if anything happened to their mates".

For what felt like the first time ever, Mary had no idea what she wanted to do. Her initial impulse was to jump in her car and drive over to their company, beat down their door, and ask if her conclusions were accurate.

Sanity, however, remained to question that impulse. She couldn't possibly appear on their doorstep and demand they tell her the "truth" purely to sate her curiosity.

Mary switched the screen of her computer off, to not distract her, and picked up her phone. She pressed the memory one button, and waited for Chloe to pick up.

Just as she started to wonder if her cousin had stepped out, Chloe answered. "Hello?"

Mary frowned, her cousin sounded distracted. "Hey, it's me. Am I interrupting?"

"You're welcome to. I'm trying my hand at painting, and—"

"Painting? I thought you had that job as a mechanic down at the garage?"

"Oh, I do. It's just so unfeminine I wanted to try something else today. So I started this picture. It's supposed to be a seascape—but it looks like a four-year-old's finger-painting session. I was just trying to think of what I'm missing when you called. What's up?"

Briefly, Mary explained about Matthew's foray into the world of hacking, and her subsequent rescue.

"Thank goodness he asked you to help. You know how terrible I am with computers. I would have made the mess worse. Are you hoping to get me to yell at him? I could, but I doubt he'd listen to me."

"No, no. It's something totally different. I accidentally opened an email. Matthew was stuck in a web and I mistook it for something else."

"Yes? What about this email?"

"The email was from one of the four brothers who run the

company. It was sent to the other brothers, and it was a section of one of their journals. It talked about the moon and its pull on him. About how they were all werewolves."

There was a short pause on the other end.

"Are you sure it wasn't creative writing? Sometimes when I'm trying to get into a character's head I write stuff down as if I really were them, to set the mood and help me see things from their perspective better, you know?"

The fact that Chloe occasionally wrote came as no surprise to Mary. Chloe was a multitalented girl who had never settled in one area. She was smart—she just hadn't found where her passion lay. Instead, she did whatever took her fancy, whenever the urge struck her. By no means was she selfish; she had a huge heart and was always there for those she loved. She just had a tendency to pick and discard working jobs with the ease some people chose hot dinners.

Mary shook herself and returned to the problem at hand.

"I don't think so. Samuel sent the email out to his brothers with the object of teasing the youngest brother. He made a huge joke out of it, stating Dominic was keeping a journal, and then called him Wolf Boy. If it was make-believe, why would Samuel tease him like that? If it weren't true, surely it wouldn't be humorous?"

Mary chewed her lip thoughtfully. What she had told Chloe made perfect sense. The thought that the four of them really were werewolves made her nervous. Surely it was all just fairy tales to frighten children on stormy nights?

"You're not going to be able to rest until you figure this out, are you?"

Mary smiled wryly. No one had ever accused Chloe of not being able to see through those she cared about. "Probably not."

"Then go out there and see them for yourself. You mentioned this guy was complaining about the number of bed partners he slept with and then discarded, right?"

Mary furrowed her brow, not following Chloe's train of thought. "Right."

"Then go out there and seduce him."

Mary's eyes widened. "What?!"

She could practically see Chloe shrug her shoulders.

"You want some answers, and he sleeps with a different woman every night. Why not seduce him, sleep with him, and ask him those questions and get your answers? It'll be a normal give and take. He gets extraordinary sex, you find out whether werewolves really exist. Seems like a fair trade to me."

Mary blinked, totally stunned. Was this her little twenty-six-year-old cousin, giving *her*, a mature thirty-five, *sexual advice*?

"Chloe, you are *not* giving me sex tips are you?"

"Of course not!" Mary wondered how Chloe seemed to appear both laughing at her and offended simply by the tone of her voice. "I'm just pointing out your options here. You called to ask for my advice, and now I'm giving it to you."

Mary wondered when her young cousin had become so wise; the kid was twenty-six, for heaven's sake. Mary rubbed her forehead, a headache beginning to pound.

"So let me get this straight. You, my baby cousin, think I should drive for hours on end, to the other side of the state, to seduce a man and blow his mind with orgasmic sex, then casually turn over afterwards and instead of playing with the usual post-coital bliss and teasing, I should just ask him if he's a werewolf?"

Chloe laughed.

"You know, when you put it like that, it sounds stupid. I'm saying go with the flow, cousin. Maybe he'll be the sort of guy you *can* just look in the eye and say, 'Hey, I heard you turn furry once a month. Any truth to that?' or maybe you can kinda search his pockets or something for a Werewolves

Anonymous card. I have no idea. All I know is you will sit out here and stew for months if you don't go and do something. So go out and search for your answers."

Mary smiled. Trust Chloe to make something as stupid as driving to the other side of the state seem simple and straightforward.

"You'd better keep an eye on that crazy brother of yours then. No telling what mess he'll get into next time."

"No problem. It's about time someone other than me got itchy feet and decided to break out and try something new around here. Heaven knows Matthew will be glued to that computer of yours forever if we don't pry him away, and it's about time you went off and did something daring too."

Mary rolled her eyes. "I do not need advice from a woman who refuses to hold a job for more than six months."

Chloe laughed.

"At least I'm living my life. You just stay holed up in your office, doing your coding stuff and chatting to your online friends. I think it's a good time for you to go on a personal road trip and explore what life has to offer. I was beginning to wonder if you had any life outside those IM rooms you stay in all night."

Mary mulled it over. She wanted to go out there, so what was holding her back? Why *not* just go with the flow for once? Making up her mind, Mary decided to act on her thoughts before she could talk herself out of them again. With that thought she decided to pack straight away.

"Okay. See you, Chloe. Keep an eye on Matthew. I'll probably call you tomorrow before I leave."

"No problem, hon. See you around."

Mary hung up the phone with a feeling of total unreality. Somehow her cousin made it sound as if sleeping with a man and then asking him if he was a werewolf would be a rational course of action.

Turning back to her lowly humming computer, she turned the screen back on, determined to dig up as much information about the brothers as she could. Dominic in particular.

As she sifted through their website, this time at a much slower and more careful pace, she found interesting little pieces of information scattered through the text. She found it amazing how much information could be left in such blasé comments one would usually overlook on a first, more casual read-through.

In their descriptions of themselves, Mary found with a bit of careful reading and piecing together, that the brothers all lived on the same piece of land on the edge of Glacier National Park. Exactly where around the enormous parkland she had no idea, but even having the Park as a reference point would be helpful.

Mary wrinkled her nose. The park was truly huge, so sifting through it looking for the right house, or houses, was totally out of the question. She smiled at the mental picture of herself knocking on each and every door asking if the Rutledge studs lived here. The police would arrest her—or the men in white coats would come for her before she had covered even a tenth of the Park.

The time passed quickly, and while Mary gathered a fair amount of detail, she couldn't find anything concrete until she came across a fuzzy digital photo of the four brothers playing in a band. It had the title "The Howlers—Our Local Bar".

The Howlers? Either she possessed a more active imagination than she realized, or these Rutledge men had a wicked sense of humor. Mary downloaded the picture, then zoomed in and out of the digital image, determined to find a clue on their location.

Finally she caught sight of a banner, declaring "The Three-Legged Stool Presents *The Howlers*".

Local bar, hmm? Shouldn't be too hard to find that place close to Glacier National Park.

Tomorrow was Friday. She could easily take the weekend off; she could even be able to stretch it to Monday, if she needed. She had plenty of annual leave stored up. The chances of finding Dominic at his local bar might be slim, but four brothers as studly as these should be well-known.

It was possible a heap of people would know where they lived. It seemed like the next logical step into finding out about Dominic Rutledge.

Mary wrinkled her nose at her desperate thoughts. Maybe she was losing her mind. Calling out to Matthew that the computer was free, she left her study and climbed upstairs to her small bedroom.

Packing a light bag, making notes about groceries and last minute errands she didn't want to forget, Mary felt strangely nervous and excited at the same time. Chloe was right, it *had* been far too long since she had struck out and done something for herself simply for the fun of it.

She decided it was stupid to worry, when the worst-case scenario was that she'd waste a weekend looking for a man she couldn't find. Or even embarrass herself in front of a man she would never see again. So what if she asked Dominic Rutledge if he was a werewolf and he thought she was insane? More likely than not, she would never see the man again, so who cared if she made a fool of herself?

So other than possible humiliation, or wasting her time, she had absolutely nothing to lose—and a potential weekend of hot sex and traveling through the state to gain.

Seemed like a fair deal to her. Particularly when she thought back to the brooding, sexy man labeled Dominic Rutledge, with the scorching blue eyes and shoulder-length wavy dark brown hair. Even on a digital image, he fairly radiated sexual energy and allure. Jumping into bed with him would not be a problem, and she certainly wouldn't have to fake anything.

Double-checking her packed bag, Mary determinedly left her room, intent on filling the rest of the day with cleaning until she could collapse in bed and sleep the hours away until she would leave. Even though she had made her decision, she didn't want to lose her nerve by dwelling on what she was doing. Deep inside her something had clicked when she had seen the picture of Dominic.

Something about all the men had seemed feral yet restrained at the same time. As stupid as it seemed, she had no trouble at all believing these men could change into huge wolves once a month.

Her impulse might be bizarre and crazy, but something in Mary knew she would never rest until she had followed this, whatever it was, through. Sure, she might make a fool of herself, but at least she would get her answers and be able to let it rest.

A determined gleam in her eye, she grabbed the polish rag and headed into her living room to do some dusting.

* * * * *

Dominic madly typed at his keyboard, determined to catch the hacker who had been stupid enough to try and break his code. While there were no state or federal secrets inside their website, Rutledge Security *did* pride themselves on having the best, the most up-to-date security and systems on hand. While nothing was hacker-proof, their systems and encryptions were as close as one could get. It was a source of incredible pride to Dominic.

Dominic's instincts warned him that the talented, but obviously gauche, kid who had started hacking into the Rutledge Security files had called in extra firepower. The initial hacker had certainly been talented, but untrained — they hadn't realized the careful snare Dom had set up and they had fallen into it like a ripe plum.

He grinned hugely at the shock and surprise the kid must have felt. The kid was good enough to break in, but not trained enough to know how to get out. Dom felt a momentary spurt of ego to know his personally created system worked.

There had been almost no action after the initial squirming, and then suddenly he was trying to follow a flurry of activity. To his well-trained eye, the new person was obviously a veteran. Slowly and meticulously the new person unwound the kid from the highly tricky snare.

Dominic unwillingly felt a rush of respect for the new person. Not only were they well-trained and quite talented, but patient as well. The confidence mixed with the patience made him wonder if the kid had called in a woman to help him. Many men would have taken the few deeper traps he set, appearing as quick-fix exits. The woman didn't rise to any of his baits.

Dominic had purposely set the trap such, in the hopes of further trapping any hackers. Also, he needed to buy himself as much time as possible to track them down. Somehow it hadn't fully worked this time.

Too busy trying to trace their Internet source and point of connection, Dominic hadn't been fazed by the new arrival trying to un-pry themselves. But the speed with which they were becoming untangling, coupled with the thought it was a woman beating his system, set his teeth on edge.

Dominic tapped his foot impatiently and resisted the urge to pace like a caged animal.

Something about this hacker, this *woman*, tugged at him. She pricked his pride, but more, she pricked his *interest*, as few women ever had.

All the details would be collected on Samuel's main computer back at Artemais' house, so he couldn't even read the data as it was collected and begin to collate it. He gave up his resistance and began to pace — restlessly, anxiously, feeling as if his hands were tied. The lack of control he held over the entire situation grated on him. It was a completely alien, strange feeling to him.

All sorts of scenarios from a kid's prank to a hardened criminal flashed through his mind. The original hacker was almost certainly a kid. The lack of experience was obvious and easy to pick out—even over the web.

It was the new person who worried him. This *woman*.

Dominic could feel himself getting closer and closer. The lady could evidently tell he was getting closer too. She now desperately struggled out of the code. Dominic felt thankful the hackers were far too busy untangling themselves to steal or read any private files. Everything was tightly locked down. Nothing had been tampered with.

The small numbers of files saved onto the communal access were nothing. They hadn't been breeched for the most part, certainly nothing had been copied from what he could tell, but even so, Dominic felt no concern for anything in an insecure area. All the important files were so heavily secured he would certainly know if they were being opened or accessed.

Yet this was mild comfort to him. His precious security setup had been breeched. By a kid, of all people!

Keeping a determined eye on the readouts flashing across his screen, Dominic was startled when an animated, voluptuous woman appeared on his screen. She was naked, with her back turned to him. Long red hair fell down to her shoulder blades, creamy white skin glowed in contrast to the silky-looking locks. Her naked ass swayed slightly as she turned to look at him.

Dominic felt his mouth dry out. *Oh man, the things I could do to that ass…*

Dominic's attention adhered to her rounded ass as it swayed. The animated woman was his every heated wet dream. Femininity incarnate. Dominic wondered if the whole setup was some sort of insane joke from his brothers.

Stunned and completely turned on at the luscious animated figure pouting on his screen, Dominic simply stared at her. Wicked green eyes glinted as the female winked at him. Pouting her lips even more, the red beauty kissed her palm, and blew him the kiss. Then she teasingly slapped her wonderfully rounded ass—a perfect size to hold on to as a man plunged himself up to the balls—winked again, and then she was gone.

Cursing a blue streak, Dominic typed a few commands, and then sat back, grumpy and defeated. Whoever the hacker was, she was long gone. Dominic rubbed his eyes, trying to contain the howl of rage and frustration he felt building up inside himself. He couldn't even explain to himself the fierce desire to catch this hacker. Something about the person who came to rescue the initial hacker had piqued his curiosity.

Now, not only was Dominic truly pissed at the knowledge that his sacred code had been broken into, but he also resented the huge hard-on he wore. The thrill of the chase, of the hunt, had sparked new life into his weary world. Other than his rampant cock, he couldn't explain why this one hacker drew him, taunted him more than any other hacker wannabe ever had.

He shut down his main computer, pounding the desk in his frustration and picked up the phone. Dialing a number without even glancing at the number pad, he turned back to his totally secure laptop, and continued to save, and make backups of all the data he had collected.

"Yo," came the answer from the other end.

"Sam? What the hell are you doing there?"

"Well, Dom, darling, tomorrow is the big birthday bash. We're *all* supposed to be down here. I presume you're still off fucking your way through the town, hmm?"

"No such luck, brother dear, I've been defending the innocence of Rutledge Security. Can you log on to Art's computer and save all the info I've sent over? We had a hacking attempt."

"No shit? Hang on."

Dominic smiled at the instant attention Samuel gave him. The surprise in his brother's tone made Dominic smile. His grin stayed on his face as he double-saved his information by burning them onto CDs, determined not to lose even a micron of his information.

"I stand corrected, brother mine. Looks like a kid, probably trying to prove his balls to his buddies. What do you think?"

"Probably, it's the second hacker that came in to rescue him I wouldn't mind speaking to. Patience of a saint, and obviously a pro. The character was hanging around somewhere, and the kid probably called him when he realized he was stuck. Maybe it was even his computer the kid was using, testing himself. Whatever, I'll want to do the coordinates and double-checks tomorrow at the party. Can you just double-save everything, in case the power goes down overnight?"

"No problem. You better not spend too much time in here, checking the details. Wills and Josie might castrate you if you're not paying proper attention."

Not only was this Sunday the full moon, but the weekend was his niece and nephew's birthday party. Alexander and Samantha, his brother William and sister-in-law Josephine's children were turning four. Plus Sophie, Art's wife, was due any day now with their third child, and he wanted to be present at the birth again.

Sophie had been swearing up and down that she was having a break after this baby was born. Christiana, their oldest, was just over four and Theodore, their second child, had recently turned two. Sophie had been constantly grumbling throughout this third pregnancy that she had spent more than half of her marriage pregnant and sick, and she had

had enough of it.

Art's head was so swollen he could barely walk through the doors of the old house, and between raising and taking care of Christiana and Theodore, not to mention Alexander, Samantha Monique, and baby Julian, William's kids, the house was never quiet, never clean, but always a lot of fun.

Dominic, as always, looked forward to returning home, not only to his small cabin on the edge of the Rutledge land, but also to his forest and family. Storing one copy of the disks safely in his desk, he carried the other set of disks into his bedroom, ready to pack for his weekend back home.

The house might always be a mess and loud, but it was still home. Art and Wills, their gorgeous wives and kids might often exasperate his loneliness, but this time would be different. This time he had a purpose, a quest, to find the hacker and hopefully the pro who not only set his teeth on edge, but also piqued his curiosity and interest as almost no one had in the last few years.

He loved his siblings and nieces and nephews, he loved his home, but the ache and frustration he often felt back there had driven him into the town on more than one occasion. This time, however, would be different. This time he had a puzzle to mull over and keep him happy and occupied.

He could hardly wait to get going.

Chapter Two
Friday Morning

ဢ

Dominic struggled, but managed to ignore the shrieking children playing in the next room. Christiana was playing "Chase" with Alexander and Samantha Monique. As with any game the children played in the rambling old house, it required much shrieking, laughter, and name-calling. The pounding of little feet on the floor meant one could track all three sets of feet, if one had that insane desire.

Christiana's little brother, Theodore, played cars and trains with his baby cousin, Julian. Julian, however, had merely wanted to eat the toy cars, boats, and trains, and thus had been banished to sit in Dominic's lap in front of the computer. After a few minutes of coddling the infant, Julian had promptly fallen asleep.

A year ago, finally driven mad by the growing hordes of their brothers' families, both Samuel and Dominic had renovated the two gamekeepers' cabins less than a mile away from the main house. A small driveway that split from the main road led up to the two cabins. Dominic's cabin was nestled fully in the woods, mostly hidden from view unless one knew where it was. He loved it as it afforded him the privacy he seemed to be growing as a need, not just a luxury he wished for. Samuel's cabin was quite a bit closer to the house, just within view of the backyard.

Both Sophie and Josephine, their sisters-in-law, valiantly tried to convince them to stay in the main house—but after watching years of marital bliss, both he and Samuel had needed their own space. Neither, however, had wanted to move from the land and forest they both loved. Therefore, they had renovated the cabins and had been living there for the last year. Most meals were an extended family deal, and everyone knew they were only a phone call, or five-minute walk, away.

For now, Julian slept peacefully on his lap. The main thing Dominic had learned about babies and kids in the last four years was the only time they were truly angelic was when they slept. Dominic shook off his musings and began typing at the laptop again. Cradling Julian in his arm, he concentrated on the code and details he was following.

Not long afterwards, Samuel entered the small study.

"Hey Dom, find anything?"

Dominic merely nodded at the sleeping infant, and smiled as Samuel shook his head. He bent his huge frame down and picked up the small boy.

"I'll put him to bed. William and Josephine are having a much needed drink. I think they're almost as exhausted as Sophie and Art after that long labor. Josephine was a big help to Sophie though—wish we'd had her around the first time Sophie was threatening to castrate us all. Be back in a minute."

Dominic merely nodded, busy scanning the details he had been looking for.

"Give little Robyn a kiss from her Uncle Dom."

Samuel snorted as he left the room.

Artemais, who had started the security firm, had always been interested in keeping his security system as beefed up as possible. As well as that, the many years he had spent in the system meant he had lots of connections with the new and upcoming technology. Samuel loved his gadgets and was often tinkering with a new toy. Between the lot of them, and William's police connections to keep them up-to-date on what was legal and what was technically illegal, their security was top-of-the-line and practically perfect.

The problem was nothing was truly perfect, and even

though they all tried to keep a low profile, some of the more clever hackers knew if they wanted a *real* challenge they should try breaking the Rutledge security. Dominic's gut told him this was what they were facing—not a criminal who wanted some of their files or information. Even though his gut instincts were rarely proved wrong, only a fool would ignore a breeched system and not react.

Dominic worked the computers for both Artemais' Security and Samuel's PI firm, keeping him more than busy during the day. He had always enjoyed sifting through code, working out what was happening, and fixing problems. That's why it had been he, and not Art, who had been alerted when yesterday's hacker had penetrated their security.

After spending nearly two hours, tracking down the internet connection and different ISP's, he finally found the address he had been searching so diligently for.

Samuel reentered the room. "Found him yet?"

"Yep, just now."

"Well?"

Dominic turned to stare at his brother. Usually calm and in control, Samuel was fairly bristling with outrage and worry. Outrage that someone would dare be better than his toys and technology, worry that it was a criminal and not the curious hacker Dominic kept soothing him with.

"You're not going to believe this, but the Internet provider for the computer the hacking was coming from belongs in the name of one Ms. Mary Dennison. Address supplied," he clicked a few strokes on the keyboard. "Hmm...that's interesting, she lives just outside of Bismarck..."

Samuel frowned.

"That's just on the state's border—right? We could drive down there and make it within ten hours. Should we cancel tonight's gig and go down there?"

Dominic shook his head. He wanted time to think this through. His gut was certain this Mary was his veteran computer woman. Now armed with a name, his brain went into overdrive fantasizing the real woman behind the animated image. He still grew hard when he remembered that luscious figure, her delectable ass, and pouting lips. Despite his annoyance at having her escape his virtual clutches, a small sense of pride also welled deep inside him.

She hadn't *beaten* him—but she certainly seemed to be a formidable opponent. The curiosity mingled with the outrage and pride at her hacking out of his traps and system made him more than interested in meeting this woman.

He particularly wanted to see if she was as luscious as that damned animated redhead. While he never had a partiality to redheads, Dominic had seduced more than his fair share. The mere thought of this particular redhead had him panting and drooling like a teenage virgin trying for his first lay.

Resisting the impulse to head into one of his brothers' bedrooms, lock the door and jerk himself off, Dominic controlled his rising lust—barely. He could feel the near-fullness of the moon calling him to the mating game he so loved. It heated his blood, set his cock rampant.

Dominic swallowed. *Man, I must need a run outside more than I realized. Get a grip, Dom. Likely this Mary is sixty and wrinkled. A hag of a woman and a red herring.*

Dominic was not naïve enough to have overlooked the possibility a false trail may have been left. The thought niggled at him. If Mary Dennison wasn't the woman he was looking for, it indicated a level of criminal activity and possible malicious intent.

"I can't tell if these details are forged or true. It could be a fake address, which worries me, but we might be jumping at shadows. Let's just let it ride for a bit, check this Mary character out quietly. We can take next weekend off, and move from there. I'll scrounge up a few old contacts and do a quiet

Internet search on her."

Samuel nodded. The sound of a walking cane entering the kitchen around the back of the house could be heard.

"Where are my birthday twins?" an old, well-known voice shouted from the back entryway.

Three pairs of feet came thumping down the hall. Childish shrieks echoed through the hallway and muffled grunts and strained noises could be heard as Christiana and the twins evidently hurled themselves into their great-grandfather's still strong arms.

"Grampa! Grampa!"

"What did you bring us?"

"Did you make us more wooden trains?"

"Mom! We wanna open the presents!"

"Edward's here!"

Samuel and Dominic rolled their eyes at each other as Christiana's voice could be heard over the twins' squeals of delight. If their grandfather had arrived, evidently so had Roland, his wife Helene and their seven-year-old son, Edward.

Roland had only recently returned from a long period of healing time with his wife and their grandfather. The brothers only knew a small amount of what had happened to the young man. Zachariah Rutledge could keep secrets like no other man alive, and in regards to Roland, he had decided to keep his own council.

All the brothers knew was that their grandfather had thought it imperative that Roland heal, be reunited with his True Mate and their young son. They had married in a small ceremony nearly three years ago and been living in the middle of the woods with the Old Man until recently.

When Edward and Christiana had met they had instantly become close friends, a strange bond none of them seemed to question, yet one none of them really seemed to understand, either.

As Dominic and Samuel made faces at each other, the thumping of little feet could be heard heading their way. Within seconds, four bundles of pure energy came crashing through the door.

"Uncle Sam! Uncle Dom! Grampa's here!"

"So is Edward!"

"They brought presents!"

"All wrapped pretty!"

Dominic smiled. At least some things were easy to see and solve. Pushing aside thoughts of the luscious redhead, and his own doubts and questions, he bent down to welcome Edward and attempt to calm his excited nieces and nephew.

Solemnly shaking the young man's hand, he welcomed him. "Nice to see you again young man. You're well?"

Edward nodded, his black curls bobbing.

"Yes, Dom. Mom and Dad have moved into a house just on the other side of town. They said we needed to be close to Grampa Zach."

Dominic smiled at the solemn little boy. Crouching down, he grinned at the young face. When Christiana started pulling at his arm, he turned his attention to his niece.

"Come on, Uncle Dom! We need to get Mom and Dad and everyone else. I wanna start eating that cake!"

"Sure thing, sweetheart. What's say we go and say hello to Grandpa first? Make him comfortable. We can put the twins' presents on the table with everyone else's gifts."

Taking a hand of each twin, he calmly led the children from the study and herded them towards the main living room. Greeting his grandfather, who looked remarkably handsome and healthy for his advanced years, he braced himself for a long, energetic afternoon.

With luck it would help him forget that damned redhead animated woman, though deep inside the pit of his chest, he knew nothing much would help. Silently, he counted the hours until the nearly full moon would rise.

* * * * *

As dusk arrives

Dominic stood on the very edge of his piece of land. Deep inside the forest, he could sense he was all alone.

At last.

Strangely, neither Art nor William had teased him over his pensive mood. Dominic didn't want to dwell on whether they could read mystical signs of what ailed him, or whether they were simply too embedded in their own marital bliss to realize he had been so silent over the course of the birthday dinner.

Only Samuel had teased and jeered at him as he excused himself early to go for a run. The kids had all been too bloated on party pies, junk food and birthday cake to want to come with him.

And so here he stood, surrounded by the dark, towering trees, letting the peace and scents of the forest he had loved all his life seep into his soul, sooth his aching pride and emotions.

Closing his eyes, he felt his form shimmer, felt the change begin to overtake him as the almost full moon rose above the horizon.

Even though he could change at will, with or without his mistress the moon, something tonight compelled him to pay homage to her once more. Maybe it was because he knew he would have to pay homage on Sunday, when she was truly full, or maybe it was simply trying to not think of Mary, or the hacker. Whatever, he knew with a strange sense of innate intuition—he needed this run and needed to clear his head.

Or maybe he just wanted to turn to his animal side for a moment, to clear his thoughts and change his perspective.

In that moment between being a man and a wolf, Dominic smiled, a large, completely masculine, toothy grin.

36

In the blink of an eye, he felt himself change to his wolf form.

He closed his eyes and inhaled deeply, as he always did in that first moment of being a wolf and gathering his bearings.

He could smell the dampness of the earth, the rich scent and tone of the soil and life beneath his paws.

He could hear the moon shimmering and calling to him, heating his blood and filling his soul with music only She could create.

He heard each insect and pad of animal footfalls on the soil. He heard the crickets chirping and the birds humming.

The earth spoke volumes to him, and he could read it all in the manner the human side of his mind could not comprehend.

Even so, he could detect the faint scent of the humans, and a small part of his mind mulled still over the conundrum of his female hacker.

His ears pricked at the sound of a rabbit crossing his path. His interest diverted, he pounced after the animal, determined to play and maybe forget his problems for a while. The earth soothed him and the moon urged him on.

Life didn't get much better than this.

Chapter Three
Saturday evening

જી

Mary sat on the edge of the bar's dance floor, playing with her light beer.

For what felt like the millionth time, she forced her doubts away. This whole escapade seemed almost too easy. The long drive had flown by, her thoughts centered on different fantasies and scenarios. In one, Dominic merely took one look at her and swept her off her feet, carrying her back to his apartment and seducing the hell out of her. In another, she could somehow magically tell by one look that he *was* a werewolf and could then seduce *him* with a clear conscience.

Overlying all of these emotions sat the eager, almost girlish anticipation of seeing Dominic in the flesh. Mary refused to think of those hours she had sat in front of her computer monitor, reading and rereading the details she found on Dominic Rutledge. She blindly ignored the restless night's sleep, the tossing and turning. The images of that cheeky, gorgeous, smiling face, and wickedly laughing blue eyes burned into her mind and deep in her soul.

She couldn't clearly remember the last time she had been so overcome by lust for a man. Her past was littered with lovers, yet Dominic was different. He seemed like a fever in her blood, a craving she could not deny.

Listening to his music, watching him, his brother, and a friend make music and seduce every woman in the bar, taught her much. The music was jazzy, soulful…bluesy tunes with huskily crooned lyrics that reached out and touched every woman present.

The choice of songs, the style of the music, and the depth and emotion the three men created showed Mary a small portion of his soul. Both it and the sexy man were too tempting to ignore.

While not precisely losing her nerve, Mary entertained doubts on the wisdom of her quest. Safely back at home, her thought of indulging in white-hot sex with Dominic, blending into his hundreds of other lovers and somehow finding out if he really was a werewolf, had seemed strange, but not unmanageable.

Now however, watching how every woman drooled over him, shrieked and cried out at his every movement, Mary had to wonder at her wisdom. It seemed insane to simply waltz up to him, smile at him, and offer him a night of no-holds-barred sex.

She took another sip of her beer to ease the dryness of her throat. Waiting for the right moment to approach him and offer her dare for one night of raunchy sex, Mary smiled as Samuel came back onto the stage.

While he was handsome and sexy, he didn't ring her bell like Dominic did. He did, however, have the lustiest, most husky, sexy, singing voice she had ever heard. His crooning words swirled around the small bar, enticing and seducing every female present.

Mary was surprised when he walked past the microphone to pick up Dominic's saxophone instead. Mary blinked, surprised, until she noticed Dominic walking up to take the microphone.

He was going to sing!

While Dominic had mostly played the saxophone, he had swapped to the guitar for a few songs. Samuel had stayed singing, until now, the last song of the night.

Lee Scott, their friend and bass guitarist for the evening, took up his spot, with Dominic taking the microphone. Drunken patrons cheered and rushed back onto the dance floor, expecting more of the quality blues and jazz they had played all evening.

Without any words or introduction, and with none really being needed, Lee stepped into the spotlight and started the instrumental. There were a few feminine cheers and shrieks — with one woman in the back screaming out *"I love you, Lee!"*

Without missing a single beat he grinned wickedly into the audience in general, his cocky grin and confidant manner earning him more whistles and shrieks, and continued the introduction. Mary recognized the tune instantly as *Night Prowler* — one of her favorite songs — and tried to stifle the sudden giggles that threatened her.

As Dominic's lusty croon washed over her, her eyes constantly met with his. The irony of the words wasn't lost on her. She couldn't put her finger on how, why or when; but with the innate intuition and wisdom only a woman could have, she realized she *knew* the truth to her question.

Maybe it was in their smiles, or the way they held themselves. Maybe it was simply the raw, earthy, completely masculine animal magnetism both men had. But in that moment, Mary knew she alone in this room understood the two brothers were *true* Night Prowlers. They were werewolves.

"Somewhere a clock strikes midnight,
And there's a full moon in the sky,
You hear a dog bark in the distance,
And you hear someone's baby cry.

"A rat runs down the alley,
And the chill runs down your spine,
And someone walks across your grave,
And you wish the sun would shine."

Mary could feel the intensity in the song, in the truth and conviction in Dominic's words. Here was the real deal. She could so easily see him slipping into the role of Night Prowler. Of stalking prey, whether animal or woman. Watching them, following them.

It was an intensely sexual image she had flash across her brain—one that seared her and simply would not leave. It was incredibly sexy and slightly scary at the same time. The mix of fear and sexiness hit the exact right note with her, making her damp and excited.

She and every other woman in the bar.

"I'm your night prowler, asleep in the day,
Yeah, I'm your night prowler — get out of my way,
Look out for the night prowler; watching you tonight,
Yes, I'm your night prowler, when you turn out the light.

"Too scared to turn your light out,
'Cos there's something on your mind.
Was it a noise outside the window?
Was there a shadow on the blind?
As you lie there naked; like a body in a tomb,
Suspended animation, as I slip into your room."

Mary shivered. Dominic was watching her, and suddenly she felt like a rabbit caught in a snare. She could feel the passion in his words, feel the man's wicked intent in his seductive croon.

With the intense way he watched her, looked at her, sought out her eyes with his, she wondered if Dominic had chosen this song purposely. To prepare her, to warn her.

The electricity, the intense connection flooded between them, snapped between them as strong as any rope or silken cord could. Mary could feel her heartbeat accelerate, could feel herself growing damper and short of breath.

An image entered her mind, herself in her small but cozy

bedroom, lying naked under the covers, while Dominic crept like a shadow, sliding into her room to seduce her. Seduce her with his words and wicked deeds. His hands, his tongue, his cock. She felt enticed, scared and enthralled all at once.

Somehow Dominic managed to dare her with this song. His eyes glinting in the dark bar, he grinned as he crooned the words to her. Despite his bad boy demeanor, despite his self-proclamation in that email of having a different woman every night, Mary could feel the intensity radiating from him. This was not a man she would want to fall on the bad side of.

Mary half-listened to the spectacular guitar instrumental by Lee, and before she realized, it was over and the saxophone was wailing its final notes. Samuel came forward and thanked the bar and its patrons. Mary blinked, and Dominic began to cross the dance floor, making a beeline for her.

Women left and right were throwing themselves at him, as more than a dozen scantily clad, clinging women converged on Samuel and Lee. None of the three men would have even the faintest problem of acquiring a bed partner—or three—tonight.

Mary dug in her purse for a tip. She couldn't put her finger on any one thing that had given the two brothers away—but she was now *convinced* they really were werewolves, stupid as it sounded.

Something, maybe her intuition, readily accepted these men turned into huge beasts during the full moon. While she didn't believe they became mindless, ravaging beasts, something inside her clicked when she looked deep into Dominic's eyes. She wanted to think this through more thoroughly.

"Can I buy you a drink? My name is Dominic."

The simple, husky words effectively froze her and muddled her thoughts. She didn't need to turn around to work out who was standing half-behind her. She could feel the heat of his body, even without the contact.

Taking a deep breath—this is, after all, what she had come for—she looked up into Dominic's face. His hair was all shaggy from running his hands through it over and over during his breaks on the saxophone. He looked rumpled and sexy, as if he had just stepped out of bed.

Mary smiled. Now that the moment had arrived, all her nerves fled. *Go with the flow*, Chloe had insisted. Well, here she was, going with the flow.

"Sure, thanks. I'm Mary."

Placing the strap of her bag back over her shoulder, she waved to the seat on the other side of her table. Dominic ordered a Scotch for himself, and a refill of her light beer. As he sat down, his legs brushed hers. A thrill of electric current passed between them. Mary had never reacted so strongly physically to a man before.

For just a moment, she worried about the wisdom of a one-night stand. Barely had the thought crossed her mind than her confidence returned. Dominic seemed like a nice enough guy. He certainly wasn't interested in anything permanent. Why not have one night of ecstatic sex while she was here? One night would surely be enough after it was over.

Mary smiled as she raised her glass in a silent toast to Dominic. He smiled and returned the toast with one of his huge, charming grins. Mary felt her heart accelerate and a warm flush spread over her body.

The night had just begun.

Chapter Four

&

Dominic did his best not to stare at the woman seated across from him. He had to remind himself constantly that she might be an enemy. Her musky, womanly scent teased and tormented him—hinting at how she would smell when creaming and open fully to him.

As this woman had such a naturally musky scent, the thought of the tang her desire could add to that musk had him nearly rabid with the need to open her to him, to have her taste on his lips and tongue. The question of whether she would indeed merely smell and taste better when aroused had left him with a permanent boner during all the sets.

He desperately tried to remind himself this woman might be conspiring against him and his brothers—to ignore the immense heat and sexual chemistry she brought to life in his body with a mere glance.

When he first entered the bar to take the stage, he had smelled her. From clear across the room the musky, taunting scent of her body reached him and grabbed his libido and guts in a fierce clench. When he finally got a clear view of her, his knees had threatened to buckle underneath him.

A pint-sized package of sex and temptation, that's exactly what Ms. Mary Dennison was. It was hard to tell exactly what height she was, sitting down at the table, but Dominic guessed she reached around five-foot-two or three.

Just like the animated woman he still dreamed about, she had long red hair that caught the lights and glinted with temptation. Even across the bar he could see her wicked green eyes that changed colors, from blue-green to the deepest of emerald greens, like the sea.

For possibly the first time ever, Dominic was trying desperately hard to control his sexual urgings. The mating game, as he liked to call the complex sexual rituals a man and woman danced through, had never seemed so challenging and interesting.

He kept reminding himself he needed to pump her for information, but his rampant cock kept insisting on another form of pumping altogether. Through all of this, the back of his brain insisted this woman had no criminal motives. Yet Dominic refused to be ruled by his cock, however lovely the outcome of following his desires might be.

The tiny part of his brain still working, the intellectual side of him insisted there must be a reason this woman sought him out here. The fact she had found him in such a short period of time proved to him she was indeed clever, and thus he needed to be wary.

Pity the thinking part of him was so small. The rest of him, hormones, cock and body were all interested in a completely different agenda. One that included getting naked and very frisky in the quickest time possible.

His lust-crazed hormones desperately wanted to pick her up, carry her out of the bar and back to his apartment. He craved to slowly show her each and every fantasy he had ever written about, ever dreamed in the heat of the night.

The longer he looked at her, sought out teasing glimpses of her, he found her even more beautiful than the animated cartoon she had used to tease him. Her breasts were a decent handful, her hair looked as soft as silk, her skin was the pale, creamy shade of a true redhead.

But her eyes...her eyes were pure temptation. They held laughter and secrets; carnal urgings and a womanly confidence in her own sexual skills were all hidden within those emerald green eyes.

Dominic smiled. Here, finally, was a woman who would challenge him. He merely hoped he could hold his lust in check long enough to find out what she really wanted from him. There had to be a reason for her visit, and he needed to know before he seduced her silly and thrust himself deeply inside her.

Everything tonight was a new spin on a previously well-worn concept of the mating rituals he underwent most nights of the week. Mary, though she obviously didn't realize it, was adding spice into his life. He merely had to remind himself she might be an enemy and to keep on his toes and his thoughts out of the gutter.

Never had the thought of questioning a woman sounded so sweet. Never had the complexities of life he adored seemed quite so enticing and arousing.

Taking a sip of his Scotch, he felt the warm amber liquid burn down his throat. With luck, he could question her in his favorite manner. He had often fantasized about teasing a helpless captive. Driving a sexy woman mad with desire and tease her to her breaking point. Never being given the opportunity, Dominic had played out other fantasies instead, following the more normal strictures of the mating game.

Yet here was his perfect opportunity.

Wondering how quickly he could lead her back to his apartment, she surprised him with her candor and boldness.

"Much as I'd love to sit here with you and have a few more drinks—what say we head back to your place?"

Usually, Dominic loved having women take control at this stage. It showed that not only were they mature enough to know what they wanted and go for it, but it also showed a confidence in themselves that was an instant turn-on for him. Amazingly, his cock hardened even more and he smiled.

"One question first, Mary; are you a criminal?"

Surprise flared in her eyes. *Fantastic*, he had caught her off-guard.

"No, I'm not. Is that a common question you ask potential

bedmates?"

Dominic carefully and slowly took another sip of his Scotch. "Not usually, no. Yet it's not usual that someone who had been inside my brothers' security files tracks me down looking like sin and temptation incarnate, either."

Dominic carefully studied his quarry. She seemed reluctant, surprised.

"A very dear friend of mine—a young acquaintance—took a stupid dare. He got stuck. I got him out. It won't happen again. End of story."

Dominic really looked at Mary. His intuition told him she was speaking the truth—just as he had hoped. Deeper questioning could come later in the evening, when his cock was sated and when he had the time and privacy to indulge in some of his harder fantasies—Mary seemed confidant enough and bold enough to be willing to follow along.

Even if she weren't willing, she didn't seem like the kind of woman who would go along with something she wasn't comfortable with. She would tell him if he pushed her too far.

He nodded, his mind made up and his cock bursting from his pants. "Fine. Shall we leave?"

He stopped when Mary put a hand on his arm.

"If you can be blunt, may I?"

Dominic paused, curious. "Of course, my dear, ask away."

When Mary leaned forward, bent her head for more privacy, looking around to make sure no one could listen in, his curiosity piqued. What on earth was she going to say?

"Are you and your brothers really werewolves?"

She asked with such caution, such sincerity he felt a smile broaden his face. He raised an eyebrow. His macho, male show of arrogance obviously unsettled her. She rushed on, "I found an old email, quite by accident. I came here because I simply had to know, would go insane if I didn't find out for sure."

"And so you came here dressed as tempting as sin to seduce the information out of me?"

Dominic could barely believe the very faint flush that rose to her cheeks. Mary certainly wasn't some virginal miss, yet he had flustered her. He idly wondered if that flush went all the way down her neck to her delectable breasts. He resolved to find out later tonight.

Taking pity on her and her strange show of bravado and awkwardness, he bent toward her and brushed a kiss along her cheek.

"Yes, love. We are werewolves. Do you still want to come back to my place?"

Dominic held still, patiently, as Mary looked carefully over him. He tried to rein in his impatience. He felt a thrill go through him as she placed her hand in his.

The electric connection between them had merely grown with their urgent questions answered. He knew Mary would want a deeper explanation and he would be happy to give her one later. Just as he wanted a deeper explanation of this very dear friend who had hacked into Art's security files.

Time enough for all those deeper explanations later. His hard-on was making him dizzy. All the blood had rushed south a number of hours ago when he first smelled Mary. He had been hard so long, he could barely walk straight.

"Let me just say goodnight to my brother, then we can be on our way."

As she nodded, Dominic stood up, still clutching her hand. He indulged himself, bent over and kissed her soft lips. The heady, musky scent nearly brought him to his knees, begging for more right there in the bar.

Taking a firm grip on himself, he made do with the simple, far too chaste kiss, and headed over to the huge crowd surrounding his brother and good friend.

Samuel and Lee were holding court among fully half the women in the crowded bar. As Samuel saw him approach, he disentangled himself from a particularly busty, clinging blonde, and started to meet him halfway.

Lee, however, with an arm around a busty redhead clinging to his neck stringing kisses along his half-bared chest, and another arm around a willowy blonde, seemed to be enjoying himself too much to do more than nod and wink.

Pulling Samuel aside, he explained he was taking Mary home with him to question her. Samuel laughed.

"Need some help, Dom? I would love to assist you. It's been a while since we...double-teamed."

Once in a while, Dominic and Samuel would both desire the same girl. If she was experienced enough, and they were in the mood, the thought of taking both brothers appealed to the girl. As a casual thing, the brothers enjoyed sharing in a threesome.

While Dominic had never minded sharing his women with Samuel, something about Mary cautioned him that he wouldn't feel so casual about sharing her. He felt a sardonic smile cross his face. Samuel seemed perplexed and Dom couldn't find the words to explain how he felt without having his brother howl with laughter and keep him hanging around even longer.

Dominic was amused to find he seemed to have a streak of possessiveness and jealousy he had never before possessed when it came to this particular woman. Explaining this to Samuel, however, would bring brotherly jeers and waste more time than he felt prepared to give.

He quickly pushed down and ignored the flare of masculine possessiveness. He was merely curious about her. She was gorgeous and he had been entertaining fantasies about her since he saw that damn animated picture of her.

He was interested in satisfying his curiosity, and having some brilliant sex with a hot woman. After he had slaked his desire somewhat, he could then ask the rest of his questions, and find out what she wanted with the records. This he could all achieve by himself—Samuel wouldn't be needed.

Sure, buddy. This has nothing to do with the fact she's hot and you're horny for her and don't wanna share.

He ignored the mocking laughter that reverberated inside his head.

"No thanks, Sam. I think I can handle her myself."

When Samuel raised an eyebrow, he felt himself flush.

"I don't think I've ever heard you turn down one of my offers for that. She special?"

"Of course not," he bristled. "I just thought that you have enough women here, I'd spare you the effort of taking so many numbers and trying to call them later on. I can handle one tiny woman all by myself."

Samuel snickered and Dominic felt himself bristle again.

"Just don't leave me the only unmated brother, okay? I'm already sick of Sophie and Josephine setting me up with every female in shouting distance. I don't need three women around in my life pushing me to mate and settle down."

Dominic raised an eyebrow.

"I'll merely be questioning her as to why her friend hacked into our security, and how she managed to get out of it. That's all."

"Friend?"

Dominic shut his mouth and glared at his brother.

Rolling his eyes and sighing, Samuel let it slide. "Whatever. Just call if you need a hand, okay?"

Nodding, Dominic returned to Mary. She was standing by their table, watching the other patrons and slowly sipping her beer. Dominic felt a large grin spread across his face. All night, heated images of ways he would question his unknowing captive had been torturing him, keeping his cock as hard as steel. With the myriad of naughty images flicking around his brain, and the huge toothy grin on his face, Dominic had never felt so much like the Big Bad Wolf.

Now and then, when a partner had broached the subject, he had dabbled in bondage. There was little in the right circumstance that he wouldn't do, and even less that wouldn't turn him on. As he drew closer to Mary, he noticed her ass was as delectable as that of the animated figure, maybe better, for this ass he could grab and use as he plunged himself into her.

She was shorter than he had expected. At six-foot even, he was the shortest of his brothers, and used to privately lament that inch or two he lacked—while publicly ribbing his brothers about the extra inch or two he had on them in *other* areas.

Drawing up next to Mary, he relished the feeling of power he felt towering over her. He felt like a conquering hero, like a warlord about to ravish the spoils of his war.

Dominic silently shook his head. His brain really needed a challenge. He had no idea just how wild his imagination could be. Maybe it was simply Mary bringing it out in him. Hastily, he discarded the thought.

Wrapping an arm around Mary, he bent down and nipped at her neck. She jumped, startled, but then melted into his embrace.

She was incredibly responsive to him. He felt his cock harden even more. This was certainly his lucky night.

"Did you drive?"

She nodded, tried to clear her throat.

"Come on, then. I hitched a lift with Sam. I'll give you directions to my apartment."

Leading them both out the door, he ignored the few women who tried vainly to catch his attention. Lost in Mary's musky scent, enjoying the faintest whiff of tang he had been sure would become more and more present as he worked on her during the coming night, Dominic barely even registered the seductive smiles and pouts of the other women.

He only had eyes for Mary as she led him to her small car parked on the street.

Giving her the easy directions, within minutes they were again pulling up to park on the street. Neither of them had said anything much beyond the directions, and he was glad for it. Feeling as though he were drowning in her scent, Dominic wasn't sure he could have coherently carried on a conversation.

Locking the car, he led her up into his den…apartment.

Chapter Five

ဢ

Mary tried to control her excitedly racing heart as she waited impatiently for Dominic to unlock his apartment door. She could barely believe how eager she was to have sex with this man.

She wasn't exactly a nun and had never pretended to be. Yet, when she thought back through her past encounters with men, her average record of uninspiring lovers didn't make her Little Miss Slut-Puppy either.

With her most important question answered — kind of — the knowledge that he was a werewolf seemed rather secondary to the night of screaming, heart-pounding intense sex she intended to indulge in.

She was determined to wallow and enjoy tonight, make a million memories that could burn in her mind for the next few months. Stories she could repeat and wickedly tell her grandchildren when she was old and alone. Stories of how she was seduced by a werewolf, stories of how *she* seduced a werewolf and had one incredible night of screaming-to-the-rooftop, excellent sex.

As Dominic opened the door, stepping gallantly aside to let her enter first, she brushed her curvy body against his much harder, muscled frame. He froze, eyes widening. Mary felt that rush of sexual energy spread across them both again. Grinning, she stepped into his neat apartment.

Dominic flicked the lights on, and Mary took a quick look around. Neat and compact, it was obvious this was not his primary place of residence. The comfy place had the feel of a summer home, or winter residence, not that of a permanent home.

Turning back to Dominic, she watched him shut and lock the door behind them. When he turned and leaned against the door, smiling sexily, she decided to take the lead. Better to be the seductress. A part of her mind considered if she could take control sexually, it would be far easier for her to leave in the morning.

She sashayed up to him and pressed her body against his lean muscles. She felt her pelvis press against his hips, aligning his iron-hard erection with her eager pussy. Just as she imagined, his cock was long and thick, definitely eager to start. Stretching up to him, she pulled his head down to meet hers.

Gently at first, she pressed her lips to his. They were soft, she found, surprised. His lips were so soft they stole her breath. Dominic uttered a low moan, heating her blood.

Eagerly, she pried his lips open and slipped her tongue inside his mouth. He was so hot inside! The damp, wet heat of his mouth beckoned to her, drew her deeper inside him. She swept her tongue over his, enjoying the slightly rough texture.

Mary wanted more. Still stretching up to kiss him, to explore his mouth, she ran one palm down his shirt, enjoying the hardness of his chest muscles, even through the thin fabric. Unsnapping his buttons, one by one, she soon had a small window of space to slip her hand inside.

"Are you the sort of girl to half finish a task?" he huskily murmured.

"Not at all." She continued touching his heated skin, teasing and taunting him. "I'm merely a girl who likes to take her time and smell the roses as I pass by. Besides," she teased him as she flicked one of his nipples, causing him to groan, "it's not as if we're in a rush, we *do* have all night, and I intend to enjoy my time, not rush blindly through it."

Mary quivered at the appreciative laugh rumbling in Dominic's chest. With her hand pressed against his warm skin, she could feel the chuckles, the muscle contractions along his pecs right down to his flat abdomen.

Mary's curiosity suddenly overwhelmed her. She needed to see this man, not just pockets of his bare flesh. She finished unbuttoning his shirt. Pulling it from his shoulders, she carelessly let it fall to the floor in a crumpled heap.

As Mary found her breath leave her body, she reminded herself she was a mature woman of thirty-five, not an eager virgin of eighteen. Dominic had broad shoulders, easily enough to bear the weight and worries of the world. His large, deep chest was perfectly muscled, not overly so like on many men who worked out too much at the gym.

His chest, just like his gorgeous face, was perfectly tanned. The deep brown sun-kissed skin flowed from his neck down over his chest all the way to his lean hips. His pants covered his body from the hips down, but Mary felt her mouth water at the thought of the continuance of both the tan and this man's splendid body. The light dusting of practically black hair over his chest made him seem more masculine—not overly hairy.

As his wicked eyes and cheeky grin proclaimed, this was certainly a model of male perfection. If the glint of laughter in his eyes were any indication, he could certainly live up to the reputation his body was declaring.

Mary firmly held the notion in her head not to drool. She didn't want to embarrass herself before her first taste of that skin, or before she could hold his rigid cock in her hands.

"Like what you see, love?"

Mary glared at him. "You know good and well any female with a pulse is attracted to your body. You're lucky you don't raise the dead with that tan and chest."

"I think you're being unfair."

"How so?" she asked, still lost in the magnificence of his body.

Dominic grinned, confusing Mary even more, for an

instant. "Here I am—shirtless and bare before you—whereas you are still fully clothed."

Mary grinned and started unbuckling his belt. "Tell you what, big boy. I'll undress you and seduce you senseless, and then you can undress and seduce me. We can take turns and cooperate."

Dominic's grin deepened, and Mary could swear she saw something wicked glint in his eye. What had he just thought of?

"Promise?"

Mary laughed, surprised at how easy it was to convince him. "Of course!"

"Then go for it, love. Just don't forget your promise when it comes to my turn."

Mary paused for a moment and then cast her doubts aside. After all, she was here voluntarily. She desperately wanted to seduce this man, to hold him in the palm of her hand and then deep in her mouth.

Hell, she wanted it all, and to do it right now. What could he possibly do to her except make her scream as she came?

Growing damp at *those* sorts of thoughts, she returned back to the task at hand. She had boasted she could seduce him, and damned if she would stand here drooling with so much beefcake standing half-naked in front of her!

Slowly, letting her hands caress each inch of beautiful bare skin they came into contact with, she began to unsnap Dominic's pants. Ever so slowly, snap-by-snap, she released his body from the cumbersome clothes. She had to grin in smug satisfaction as Dominic quickly toed his shoes off, more than eager for her ministrations.

The tan does indeed extend all the way down, she mused. *His flat abdomen, his slim hips, all perfect and divine.*

So very carefully, Mary pulled the pants down his long legs, revealing vivid, fire engine red boxer shorts.

Unexpectedly, there were no lewd suggestions on the shorts. If she had to guess, she would have expected something like "I'll hose you down" or "Firemen leave 'em wet" printed on the sexy shorts. Yet there was nothing on the shorts. Merely a taunting bulk proving it's what is *in* the shorts that counts.

As Mary bent down lower to remove his shoes and help him step out of the pants, she looked up the length of his body to stare at his face.

His face had flushed, his eyes looked wild, and Mary had a sudden image of how she must look to him. With her red hair falling around her shoulders and her breasts trussed up in a black lace bra and very low-cut red top, he would have a perfect view down the depths of her cleavage.

She grinned wickedly, enjoying the momentary vision of how he must see her, practically kneeling in front of him in the supplicant's position, breasts up in offering, her face right in front of his huge cock.

As Dominic hastily kicked aside the pants, Mary revised her plans. She had been going to drag him into his bedroom and have her wicked way with him, but something about the heat and glitter in his eyes had her rethinking her plans.

She knelt fully on the carpeted floor, catching her balance by grabbing the back of his thighs. She felt a momentary spurt of pride as surprise flared in his eyes. Surprise and heat. Having one up on this man was fun, but more, a challenge she adored.

"Mary—"

"Shhh…" she soothed, carefully pulling down the elastic waistband of his boxer shorts.

With barely a whisper of sound, they fell to the floor. They were a surprising, bright splash of color against the blackness of his pants and shirt.

Mary tried hard not to gape as his cock sprang free. Heavy and thick, it exceeded all her midnight fantasies and dreams. He stood proudly at attention, declaring for all the world to see how she affected him. For just a second she wallowed in the knowledge that *she* could turn him on, that *she* had brought this reaction to him—not some other skinny bimbo whom he would screw senseless and forget the next morning.

Teasingly, she puffed her hot breath over him, enjoying the slight twitches her heat brought to his cock. She could swear he was still growing thicker and longer, but up so close it could just be a part of her imagination.

"Mary—" he groaned, obviously reaching the point of no return.

Mary smiled. "Yes?" she panted, letting the heat of that one word flow over his cock. She licked her lips, moistening them as she looked up into Dominic's eyes.

He could tell she was letting him watch her prepare herself to take him deep inside her mouth.

Drawing out that last moment until she knew he was about to drag her head closer to him, she smiled. "Are you safe?" she inquired, half listening but too eager for him to be truly worried.

"Yes, totally, will show you the doctor's certificate later if you want. Just *please*—"

Quickly, she leaned forward, swallowing as much of him as she could without gagging. The hoarse shout from Dominic spurred her on. Sucking hard, she bobbed her head, taking more of him. Arching her eyebrows, she watched the play of emotions cross his face.

Surprise, pleasure—and then a fierce restraint.

Mary swiped the tip of his cock with her tongue. Reaching her hands up, she began to fondle his balls.

"Oh, shit—" he choked, clasping his hands to the back of her head.

Mary gently rolled his balls with one hand, while stroking the little bit of his shaft she couldn't swallow with her other. Fisting him, pumping him, she worked him into a wild, reckless frenzy. Quicker and quicker she moved on him, pleased to feel him cant his hips so he thrust deeper into her mouth.

As she worked, the sounds of his moans and that unique slurping sound that only oral sex can produce filled the air. Mary constantly looked up to Dominic's face, eager to see his pleasure radiating from him, enveloping him as she sucked on him.

She swirled her tongue over his tip, enjoying the salty tang of his pre-cum. As she felt his balls tighten and rise slightly, Mary continued to pump him, wanting to thrust him over the orgasm that sat just out of reach for him.

As Dominic started to cry out, he tightened his hands in her curls. His head thrown back, eyes closed in ecstasy, he grabbed the back of her head, pulling her even lower down his shaft. His hips pressed forward, desperate to thrust deeper inside her. She smiled and relaxed her throat muscles, as eager to swallow him as he was to be swallowed.

Still gently rolling his balls, she could feel the hardness grow in them until he finally cried out, spewing jet after jet of scalding hot cum down her throat. She easily swallowed the familiar, slightly bitter taste of cum, gently sucking him as his thrusts became less urgent and less deep.

When she had wrung him dry, she licked his tip a few more times, just to tease.

Pulling away from him, she sat back on her haunches and grinned. Still fully clothed, she enjoyed the sight of his masculine beauty, the slight sheen of sweat covering his tanned body.

Feeling a bit like the cat who swallowed the cream, both literally and figuratively, Mary grinned up at her lover. He grinned back at her, a wicked, evil, devil-may-care grin that promised untold passion in the night to come.

"Well, that was a pleasant, surprising appetizer, love.

What say I carry you into the bedroom and we can begin the entrée? I do believe it's my turn to undress and seduce you, now that you have so kindly released the worst of my pressure."

Mary grinned. It seemed like Dominic was serious about a tit-for-tat system. Now that she had pleasured him, it was his turn to pleasure her.

While she had no worries at all about them both giving and receiving pleasure, she was still determined to ultimately stay in control of tonight's sexual odyssey. She had no desire to leave tomorrow morning with a broken heart. She was a well-versed, experienced woman. She was sure she could hold her own against this stud muffin of a werewolf.

Chapter Six

ဢ

Dominic tried not to grin with delight as he helped Mary to her feet. He looked at himself, amused at how his flaccid, totally blown away cock desperately tried to raise its head. Mary had certainly surprised him with her impromptu blowjob.

He had, of course, received more blowjobs than he could possibly count over the years; but something about having Mary kneeling at his feet, in the age-old posture of supplication, sucking away at his meat, got him harder than he had ever been before.

With everything she did, every gesture she performed, his Mary seemed to up the stakes in this delicate dance, this mating game they were playing.

With her musky scent enveloping him, and that tangy smell of her cream mixing with her scent, she drove him wild. It made him feel as free as he did while running in the woods, paying homage to his mistress the moon. It shattered him and blew his mind away.

With the edge off, he could now start his plans, albeit a tad later in this game than he had intended.

Something about this woman drove him nuts, made him forget all his carefully laid plans and throw caution to the wind. While being reckless was nothing precisely new to him, Mary seemed to bring an element of the unknown into every situation with her. She was a conundrum, a wild card. And he loved it.

Life would certainly be more than interesting with her around.

His mouth watered at the thought of how he would stretch her, fit so snugly within her tight passage he could feel their hearts beating in sync with each other. He relished the challenge of her, the questions he would ask, and the new and surprisingly important mating game he would begin tonight.

The way she had taken him within her mouth, had relished sucking him, showed his beleaguered brain that she liked being in control. He could tell she liked calling the shots. He grinned in pure masculine delight. It was always far more fun to dominate someone who enjoyed the feeling of security control gave them.

Not only was it far more of a challenge to dominate a strong-minded female, but the surprising and uninhibited responses one got from these women were far richer and deeper than that of a normal submissive partner.

Smiling wickedly, Dominic resisted the impulse to strip her there in his living room. Gently leading her with his firm grip on her arm, he took her through into his big bedroom.

Shutting the door behind them, he leaned back against it. "Go over to the bed."

He struggled desperately not to laugh at Mary's mockingly raised eyebrow. He wondered for a moment if he would need to remind her of their deal—tit-for-tat. He hadn't questioned anything she did to him, now it was time for her to follow his lead.

He watched Mary quietly; let her look him up and down in his naked state, proving to her how he had followed her lead. With a short nod of her head, she followed his command and walked over to the enormous king-sized bed.

She paused saucily beside its edge, only following his literal command. Obviously she intended to make him work for every inch he could get.

Ah, the challenges she presented. *Let the mating game begin*, his brain mocked. The night stretched before him, taunting him with how much he could share with Mary, with the pleasure they could both get. Never had a woman appealed and challenged him like this one.

He pushed aside the very rampant male part of him that wanted to brand her here and now, mark her as his, and take her in every conceivable way. Dominic halted that train of thought.

One only marked one's mate…she couldn't possibly be that woman for him! Forcefully, Dominic cast aside the thoughts, willing himself to wallow in the game as he always had.

"Remove your shirt."

Slowly, inch-by-inch, she lifted her arms to the hem of the midriff top. Raising the shirt an inch at a time, she teased and taunted him with the exposure of her pale flesh. Dominic licked his lips, his control starting to slip.

Since being a teenager he had recognized his weakness for female flesh. He was a dedicated breasts man—but he loved every inch of every woman he met. Breasts, soft stomachs, thighs—particularly when they were spread for him and he could rest between them—necks and shoulders, backs and always, *always* he was up for a luscious ass. He enjoyed licking, nibbling and simply exploring every inch of a woman's form.

"The bra…"

Clearing his throat, Dominic hoped he didn't sound too much like a dying man. Mary grinned, and bent her arms back to unclasp the scrap of black lace some devious salesperson had convinced his Mary passed for a bra.

Even as she unveiled her beautiful, full breasts to his gaze, Dominic inhaled her scent deeply. There was just something about Mary's musky scent that drove him wild; something about her silky soft hair and pale, satin-soft skin that he couldn't resist. Deep inside himself, he knew she would be branded into his heart and soul forever.

As Mary teasingly exposed her bountiful breasts,

removing the black lace and spilling her creamy mounds into her own small hands, Dominic knew one night simply wouldn't be enough—for the first time in more years than he cared to think about.

He paid no attention to the cheeky top, nor the black lacy scrap that had fallen crumpled to his floor. Too busy concentrating on the skin he desperately craved like a drug, the scraps of clothes were forgotten the instant they were removed from her luscious body.

"Now the pants."

Dominic cursed his stupidity as Mary bent down to unbuckle her shoes, to kick them off before removing her black hipsters. The action of her bending down squeezed her breasts even closer together, deepening the already impressive cleavage to his view and swinging enticingly.

Dominic's cock stood up straight at attention—more than ready for some action.

Buck naked, he knew as soon as Mary righted herself to slip the hipsters over her hips and ass she would see his state. When that knowing, feminine grin came to her face Dominic reminded himself he needed some answers. He had planned to take his time here—to tease her, to taunt her. He had wanted to drive her to a fever pitch, ask her questions about who and why she had helped a petty criminal out of their system.

Yet all he could think about was his hungry cock, about thrusting balls deep into her tight, wet flesh. If he took her here and now, just like his imagination showed him in vivid detail, if he thrust himself into her over and over until they both fell asleep from the exhaustion, he would never find the answers he sought.

So he restrained himself and cursed his unruly cock. Never had he needed to hold himself back. All three of his brothers had teased him, saying he needed more restraint—more control over himself and his urges. Now wouldn't they laugh to see him eager as a schoolboy, practically spilling his seed on the carpet in his desperation to enter this particular woman?

Taking her own sweet time—obviously knowing exactly the reaction her stripping caused him—after what felt like an age Mary stood up. Clad only in her wispy set of panties she looked like his favorite wet dream. The high cut made him wonder if it were actually a thong.

Shit. He loved thongs.

"Turn—" He cleared his throat, wishing for a glass of water. "Turn around, show me your back."

With a saucy grin, showing she knew exactly the predictability of his thoughts, she obligingly turned around, showing him her luscious, perfectly rounded ass. Taunting him even further, just like her animated image from their computer play, she wiggled her ass at him.

Swaying gently from side to side, he felt as if she hypnotized him. When she looked back over her shoulder, her hair a fiery mass of curls, her ass so delightfully rounded, encased in the skimpy black thong, he worried his cock would burst.

Damn. A thong. The Goddess has got to be smiling on me tonight.

Even with the tiny scrap of lace, the thong framed her ass to his view. The teasing bit of material nestled happily between her cheeks, taunting him with how soft and tender her flesh would be, how sweet and hot her ass was. He could imagine sinking his teeth so gently, yet firmly, into that soft flesh. He could smell the tangy musk emanating from her weeping cunt. He felt his mouth water at the thought of lapping up those juices.

Closing his eyes a moment, Dominic mentally brought up his and Samuel's concerns about the security of their site. She was somehow involved with a hacker. He needed to know about her association with the kid who had made it into their system. Hell, for all he knew it could have been her son! He glanced once more at her hands. No band circled her finger.

Not even the thought of her with another man's children could deplete his lust for her. His cock couldn't care less. She was a delicious female with an ass he could happily sink his teeth into, breasts he could barely restrain himself from suckling, and a mane of long red hair he wanted running all over his body.

Reining in his control, swearing someone would pay for the restraint he had to employ to function even at this base level, Dominic attempted to calm himself down.

"Climb on to the bed," he croaked and wished to hell he could clear his throat without seeming like an eager virgin about to spill his seed for the first time.

Huge grin in place, Mary climbed onto the bed—on all fours. Shit, how could she know that was one of his favorite positions?

Again, mental images danced in front of his eyes. Mary, bound on his bed, up on all fours. Him, naked and hot, behind her, holding her ass in his huge hands. He could see himself thrusting into her over and over until they both collapsed from exhaustion, or had fucked themselves raw. Either way it didn't matter.

She would be wet, tight. He could smell her musky scent; taste her juices as they covered them both. He would plunge into her over and over and over...

Get a grip!

Dominic blinked and tried to focus. The scarves were under his pillows, the toys were in the large chest of drawers next to the bed. Somehow a scene that, previous to tonight, had slightly repulsed him now had his mouth watering in anticipation, had him hard as a rock and hoping to make it through without losing control.

By now, Mary had posed herself in one of the classic centerfold positions. Legs tucked half underneath her ass, lying back amongst the pillows, arms crooked behind her head as if she hadn't a care in the world. In the scanty black lace, red hair softly falling around her, pale skin shining, she could easily be gracing any number of magazine covers come to life.

Dominic swallowed and swore he would feast on every inch of that delectable flesh—after he had his answers. He loved Samuel to bits and couldn't possibly face him if he didn't have the answers they both sought. Playtime could come after he had satisfied his curiosity.

Wishing to hell his cock was as reasonable as his brain, Dominic prayed harder to the Goddess than he could ever remember doing.

Oh mistress, he pleaded, *give me strength.*

Chapter Seven

ை

Mary lay back in the huge bed, thinking furiously. *You schmuck! Why the hell didn't you ask him about being a werewolf when you had the chance?*

Mary took a deep breath. Being honest with herself, she knew not a single thought of asking questions had crossed her mind. She had enjoyed sucking him, touching his hot skin, fondling him so much all thoughts of asking him questions had flown from her mind.

Even if she *had* thought to ask questions, with her mouth so deliciously full of his cock, how could she have managed it? Anyway, she *did* know he thought he was a werewolf, it's just knowing that brought up a million other questions.

Being even more honest with herself, would she have *chosen* to ask questions if it meant taking her mouth away from that huge cock?

Mary squirmed. From the heat of her skin, dampness of her pussy, the desire rolling through her blood like a wave, she worried the answer would be a resounding "no"!

She did, however, feel a measure of relief seeing the intensity of heat and desire coursing through Dominic's eyes. By the look of things, he was just as helpless in his lust as she was in hers. Even though Dominic had answered her major question, admitting he was a werewolf, so many smaller things needed clarifying. Did he become a raving killer when he changed? Could silver bullets really harm him? Did he heal fast like werewolves of myth?

Despite the multitude of questions rolling through her mind, a few things she simply knew from instinct. The werewolves of myth held nothing when compared with reality.

She grinned.

Dominic and his brothers were all studs. No overly hairy, half-mad men here. While Dominic had a nice amount of hair on his chest, it was lightly sprinkled, arrowing cheekily down to his huge, erect cock. His eyes were smiling, wickedly glinting deep blue, not a wide, mad flaming red.

No, this was not the slobbering, raving madness of the old movie werewolf. This was an intelligent, sexy man, who somehow became a wolf. Even from the small snippet of journal she had accidentally read, Mary knew Dominic was fully conscious of his thoughts and decisions while in wolf form.

Hadn't he mentioned paying homage to his mistress the moon? Of feeling wild and free? Of scenting the forest and rich night air? None of that added up to a deranged, deluded killer beast.

As Dominic took a step toward her, she felt a thrill of lust course through her pussy. Beautifully naked, hugely erect, he was every woman's fantasy incarnate. His deep blue eyes held wicked secrets of hot nights and hotter acts. His smile was smug and full of male knowledge. He *knew* he could satisfy her, knew a million ways to bring her to climax. Mary licked her dry lips. She hoped they could make it through a number of those ways before they both fainted from exhaustion and sexual satiation.

Dominic rested one bent knee on the edge of the bed. Mary held her centerfold position, grinning her encouragement. He leaned over to her, pulled her legs out to lay them flat. She wiggled, enjoyed the feeling of blood circulating back in her limbs.

Mary caught her breath as Dominic came over her, caging her with his huge body. His weight rested on his arms and legs, yet she could feel his presence, feel the heat pouring from his body. Mary opened her mouth slightly, silently asking for a kiss. Wanting to feel his soft lips against hers again.

When he bent down, she felt a thrill of pleasure course through her. Maybe she *could* stay in control and still act submissive. When she felt Dominic's lips press oh-so-softly against hers, she wound her arms around his neck in glee. Arching up into him, she pressed her breasts into his warm chest.

Vaguely, she noted his hands fisted and thrust under the pillows near her head.

"Now, now, little Mary. Did I tell you to move your arms?"

Mary groaned at the removal of his warm, soft lips. She lifted up, determined to kiss him just one more time, but Dominic backed away.

"For that, I think a punishment is deserved."

Mary frowned.

"Punishment? I don't do pain, Dom. Not for you, not for anyone."

"Who said anything about pain, love? I was thinking more of delayed pleasure."

Mary blinked as he pulled out a satin scarf from under the pillow.

"Uh…"

"Tit-for-tat, love. I have a few questions I must answer before I let myself go and forget everything in your delightful body."

Mary blushed slightly, but removed her arms from his neck. She might have forgotten to ask what was on her mind, yet it didn't appear Dominic would have the same problem.

Seeing the amusement in his eyes, Mary firmly resolved not to be so besotted next time. For now, she could answer his questions, and hope he could rebuild the all-consuming fire that moments ago had been burning inside her. For her part, once Dominic had had his fun, the tables would turn once more.

Mary pressed her lips together to stop the pout she could feel forming. Next time she would ask questions first, and take her pleasure second. Let's see how the big stud felt when it was her turn to give *him* a little "delayed pleasure"!

Annoying beast, she huffed silently to herself as she deigned to let him tie her wrists in the silky scarf and attach her to his headboard.

Chapter Eight

❧

Taking surprising care, Dominic began to wrap the length of silk around Mary's wrists. After instructing her to hold onto the metal bed frame, he wound the length in a cross fashion around her wrists, taking particular care not to cut off her circulation. Now knowing how long this particular fantasy might take for him to play out, her care and wellbeing was utmost in his mind.

Having never actually played serious bondage games before, Dominic felt his excitement rise a little, even as a part of his brain wondered at his sanity. This was something new, something fresh. Yet it also was something that before tonight he had only idly wondered about, not felt this burning need to try.

It didn't take a rocket scientist to work out how these sorts of games were played, yet it brought a thrill to his chest, and more importantly his cock, to be so fully in control of his partner. He found it amusing that Fate had played him such tonight.

He had been determined to try and find a woman to pick up, with whom he felt even a modicum of curiosity about, and to begin his dabbling with such games tonight. Seconds after smelling and finding Mary, he knew he not only had incredible luck in having her arrive tonight, but also his urgent *demanding* desire to attempt such games with her burned and throbbed inside him.

He couldn't believe his luck when he had not only found Mary, but found such a desirable, delicious bed and play partner for the night.

The physical reaction Mary showed him proved she

wasn't entirely opposed to this game either. There was a very faint flush over her chest, her nipples looked painfully hard. Her eyes had that half-glazed look most women got when seriously aroused. Her cheeks were flushed and the very faintest sheen of sweat shone on her forehead.

Oh yeah, Mary was hot. Dominic rested above her, his weight distributed on his arms and legs as he crouched above her. Taking his own sweet time, he closed his eyes. Surprised, he found his mouth watering in anticipation.

Giving himself a minute, he let his senses adjust to the lack of visual stimulation. When his hearing clearly picked up the difference between his own steady breaths, and Mary's slightly accelerated breaths, he let his other senses wander.

The sheets beneath him were slightly warm and crisp. The heady scent of musk and desire filled the room. He lowered his head, eyes still firmly shut, and paused, a few inches away from Mary's delectable skin.

Feeling his mouth truly start to water, afraid he would disgrace himself and begin to drool, he reined in his control.

Taking a deep breath, he fully took Mary's scent into his body. The myriad of different scents and textures that added up to pure her. The musk, the salty tang of her slick skin, the dewy scent and flavor of her juice. The plain but wonderful scent of her soap, her herbal shampoo. Everything that together, added up into Mary.

He took her scents deep into his heart, into his very soul. She was perfect, delicious, and he would enjoy every second of eating her all up, literally and figuratively.

Letting his eyes open partially, enough to see her, yet not enough for the brightly burning lamp to hurt his eyes, he slid his glance over her flushed face. Her eyes were bright with lust and excitement. Slowly, taking his time, he moved his body downwards, until he could stare at her thong-covered pussy. Taking his time, he drew the thong down her hips and off her legs, tossing it behind him.

Her fiery red curls partially hid her from his heated view. With one finger, he gently parted her lower lips, slicking her juice around her opening and exposing her soft inner flesh.

Down here she was delightfully pink, an interesting contrast to her very pale skin. Her opening tightened, sucking at his finger as he gently inserted it into her. He stroked her walls, enjoying the damp heat of her inner self. He had to grin at the sucking, slurping noise as he removed his finger, nearly drowned out by Mary's moan of disappointment.

"Dom…" she panted.

Now that his eyes had adjusted back to the light, Dominic looked back at his bound captive, his lover, his *woman*. Suppressing the possessive, totally non-him thought, Dominic returned to his perusal of Mary.

With her arms raised above her head, her breasts thrust temptingly out, begging him to be suckled and nibbled on, Mary looked positively divine. Her eyes were closed, her head resting back on the pillows. Her legs shuffled, trying to ease the tension growing between her thighs.

Dominic grinned. She hadn't seen anything just yet.

Turning back to her luscious, weeping pussy, he gave in to his own temptation, and took a long, long, luscious lick. Mary's thighs shuddered. Her muscles clenched, and she pushed her hips up, trying to get closer, silently begging for more.

Dominic knew the slight roughness of his tongue would enhance the wet pleasure she felt. He slowly, teasingly, started to lap at her juices, careful to avoid her clit and the very sensitive outer edges of her lips.

Licking and sucking up her sweet yet salty nectar, Dominic took his own time and allowed himself to wallow in the pleasure her taste and scent brought him. He found the more he tasted her essence, the more he craved it. Like the worst addict, he had to tighten his hold on his own hunger, his own selfish desire, and concentrate on bringing Mary some pleasure too.

Slowly, he began to build the pace. His licks grew longer. Encompassing her whole opening, he began to tease her clit with the rough edge of his tongue. Slowly but surely, he built Mary into a desperate frenzy.

When she was pushing up onto his face with all her leverage, when her moans grew deep and frantic, he finally speared his whole tongue into her.

Mary cried out.

Dominic reached up, and spread her legs even further apart with his large hands. Pushing them far to each side, he lifted her legs to cant her hips even higher.

He began to eat her in earnest. Nibbling on her so-soft flesh, running his tongue over her throbbing, erect clit, Dominic gave her true pleasure. Bringing one hand away from her leg, Dominic thrust two fingers easily inside her, crooked his finger and rubbed her G-spot as he growled against her clit.

The stimulation against her previously unfound G-spot along with the vibration against her clit threw her over the edge.

Mary threw her head back deeper into the pillows, moaned deep in her throat and let loose a cry of release.

Dominic enjoyed her shudders, briefly wished it was his cock, instead of his fingers, being gripped so tightly by her sweet cunt, and lapped up the juices flowing freely from her.

He waited until her contractions ceased and she shied away from his lapping at her clit, showing her oversensitivity in her post-climactic state. He pulled his fingers from her, and slowly licked them clean. Closing his eyes, he focused on her breathing. Not as deep as when she climaxed, though still fairly rapid, he decided she had properly come down from her climax.

Ignoring the burning ache in his own cock, he promised

himself full satisfaction after the questions and the next joy for her he had planned.

Reaching up, he double-checked she hadn't hurt or chafed her wrists pulling against the restraint. While he had made sure it was a silky satin scarf, it wasn't really a weak, easily torn material, as he wanted it strong enough to restrain her.

He ran his smallest finger underneath the bind, making sure there was a little moving room for circulation. Mary smiled up at him, dazed.

"That was lovely. Is it my turn?"

He kissed the tip of her nose.

"Oh no, not yet. That was only Part One of my plan."

Mary frowned.

"What happened to tit-for-tat?"

"Well, my dear, I figure once I let you out of those restraints I won't easily get you back in them. Don't fret. You'll love this even more."

Mary pouted, but he moved away from her before she could start to argue.

Scooting across the large bed, he bent down to open the chest of drawers. Rummaging around amongst the furry handcuffs, assorted dildos, tins and packages, he finally found the bottle he had been searching for.

Dr. Dare's Womanly Sensitizing Liquid.

Samuel had bought it for his last birthday and given it to him with a huge feral grin. Artemais and William had nearly choked laughing. Dominic had merely thrown it in with all the other toys and paraphernalia he had collected over the years, thinking that maybe one day he would find a use for the liquid.

He made a mental note to thank Samuel for aiding his cause with Mary.

With his back still to Mary—no point in giving his whole game away before he was ready—he unscrewed the lid and broke the safety seal. He felt Mary stiffen next to him as the unmistakable sound of breaking plastic echoed in the room.

"Uh... I did mention I don't like pain—didn't I?"

Dominic turned around and showed her the gaudy red and yellow label.

"You certainly did, my dear. I also pointed out I wasn't into it either, that I prefer delayed pleasure." He tried to hide his grin at Mary's skeptical look at the bottle.

"Sensitizing liquid? Where on earth did you find that, a kid's joke shop?"

Dominic laughed. "No such luck, darling. Samuel bought it for me, from a very expensive adult catalogue. It might look childish and garish, but one really mustn't judge a book by its cover. I'm sure you've heard of anesthetic cream?"

He paused, waiting for Mary to nod.

"Well, this is similar, but it's edible, quite tasty from what Samuel said, and instead of anaesthetizing your...body parts, it sensitizes them, prepares them. It will heighten your own arousal, and make even the gentlest of my touches that much hotter."

Desperate to begin, Dominic nevertheless spared a brief moment for safety's sake. Squirting a small amount onto his inner wrist, he tested the cream on himself.

Having helped feed his numerous nephews and nieces, he knew how important it was to test bottles against his inner wrist before a feeding. While he trusted Samuel with his life, and knew he would never knowingly give him something dangerous to try on a lady, neither did he want to blindly assume there was no hidden catch Samuel hadn't warned him of.

After a few seconds, the patch of skin felt warm. Dominic could feel his own blood pumping under his skin, could feel the tingling sensation of his skin becoming more sensitive. There was a very faint burning sensation, but it was a heat style of burning, not an itchy or irritating style of burning.

The cream was perfect for what he intended for Mary.

He let Mary look at the small patch of skin on his inner wrist — to prove it was safe.

"No irritation, no harmful burning sensation. You know I wouldn't knowingly do anything to hurt you, love."

At Mary's cautious nod, he squirted a dollop of the cream onto her still-peaked nipple. He stared at the cream as it slowly slid down her nipple and over her rounded breast. Unable to merely watch, he reached out and gently massaged it into her soft skin.

Mary arched her back and moaned — at the gentle massage, or the warm heat of the cream he was unsure. The spot on his inner wrist still tingled. It seemed to soak up the heat of his skin, seemed to feel the heat radiating from Mary's breast.

Dominic upturned the bottle again, to anoint her other nipple. Flicking the cap back on, he let the bottle rest beside their bodies for a moment. Idly, he glanced down at the truly garish label.

600 ml – Extra Large bottle, for more fun! he read. *Fantastic. More fun for everyone.*

Grinning happily, he set to work with his hands, now covered in the sensitizing cream. The heat seemed to radiate between them, from his hands through to her breasts and back to him again. He intended to massage her until neither of them could cope anymore.

He had always been good with his hands.

Chapter Nine

&

Mary tried her best not to squirm. The aching hunger growing inside her was astounding. She'd had lovers before. Many lovers, though never more than one at a time, and somehow never falling down the slippery slope of slutdom, or becoming uncaring of whom she shared herself with. She even knew how to pleasure herself, when the run between lovers grew too long. She preferred the heated thrusts of a man between her thighs, but upon occasion when she simply couldn't bear it, she knew how to wield a vibrator quite decently.

Yet never before had she *burned* like this. Never had she felt every ripple of rough skin against her own much smoother skin. Never had the friction between herself and said lover been so unbearably sweet and desperate.

Dominic seemed to know instinctively when to be rough and when to be gentle. When the cool bedroom air on her heated flesh would make her burn hotter, and when his own hot breaths puffed across her sensitized skin would be most effective.

When he took her aching nipple into his mouth she screamed with the pleasure.

There was much to be said for Dominic Rutledge's sexual skills. Here was definitely a man who knew his sexual games.

Mary moaned, twisted, pleaded and begged. Higher and higher Dominic worked her, touching, caressing, teasing her body and senses with everything he could. And just as Mary knew she could take no more, just when she instinctively knew she would have to climax or explode—he pulled back.

"What the…? Dom, finish this!"

"Now, now, my dear. How about you answer a few very simple questions?"

Mary tried to focus. Through the haze of her thoughts, her lust-crazed mind, she recalled vaguely not only that her hands were tied, but that she was at Dominic's mercy. The thought that he would repeat his teasing, drive her even further up to that peak without giving her release was enough to make her whimper. Whether in desire or frustration she had no idea.

"Whaddya wanna know?" she mumbled, happy to answer anything to feel the release her body craved.

"Who hacked into our site?" he breathed into her ear. He was so close to her she could feel the heat of his skin, smell her own tangy juices on his lips. It was incredibly erotic and frustrating at the same time.

"M'cousin...jus' a kid...dared by friends...sex now?"

Mary held her tongue. She would *not* beg and she would certainly not whimper...or not any more than she already had.

"Your cousin, hmm? I suppose when he got caught in my snare he called you in to get him out?"

She simply nodded.

"Do you think he'll be tempted to do it again? With someone else instead of us?"

Mary shrugged. "He's bored." She cleared her throat—determined to stop sounding like a drunk kid testing herself with a first drink of beer.

She tried to continue. "He's just a kid on school break. He's good, very good, but bored. I've been trying to bully him to get a job, but no one will treat him seriously when he hasn't even started college. So he lets his friends dare him into doing stupid stuff. He's not a criminal; he's simply a talented, bored kid. Is that all?"

"One more thing. How did you find out about us being werewolves?"

"I opened an email by accident. Thought it was a portal. Was from Samuel to you and your brothers. A teasing note about a journal entry of yours he'd found. Evidently someone had saved it outside your firewalls."

Dominic nodded. He seemed to know exactly what she was talking of. "I'll fix it Monday. Thank you for answering my questions, love."

When Dominic put his hands back on her excruciatingly sensitive nipples, Mary nearly screeched.

"I'm sorry if I offended you with my timing by stopping. If I had let us continue much further I wouldn't have been able to stop, and we'd be back to your turn. My curiosity is sated, for now. It's more…physical cravings I wish to satisfy right now."

Mary moaned, unable to articulate the *about* frickin' time, mental comment she wanted to verbalize, as his hot lips took her nipple deep into his wet mouth. With a fierce determination, he continued rubbing the sensitizing liquid all over her breasts, her soft stomach and up her shoulders.

Within moments she was climaxing fiercely.

Without even a pause to let her catch her breath Dominic was starting all over again. Over and over he brought her to release. Sobbing, she demanded he fuck her.

"I want to feel your thick cock riding inside me! Please, Dom!"

"Yes!" he growled fiercely, sheathing himself deep inside her with one fierce thrust to his balls.

Yet again, Mary felt the urgency start deep in her stomach. It grew and grew, as if it had a mind of its own. A huge bundle of energy, a fierce longing and shaking, nestled deep inside her stomach and womb.

When Dominic ever-so-lightly flicked her clit, thrusting his cock so deeply inside her she marveled he fit, she felt the huge bundle erupt inside her.

Screaming her pleasure, crying and digging her nails into her hands with the desire to hold him close, Mary came for the last time. She felt Dominic's hot seed spurt deep inside her, filling her and branding her.

As the intense feelings simmered down, she fell back into the pillows, sweating and shaking. Her eyes closed, she vaguely felt Dominic reach up to untie her hands. Subconsciously, she felt him lie beside her and pull the covers up over them, but in reality she was deeply asleep.

So this is what it feels like to be fucked to exhaustion, she dimly thought.

Mary thought she was smiling, but whether it was her dream self or her thoroughly fucked self, she had no idea. She sensed herself falling down, down into the bed, or maybe it was into the earth?

Dreams rolled past her, one after the other until they seemed to merge into an almost kaleidoscope of moving pictures. Somehow they all managed to be different, yet the same.

A wide-open forest, the darkest green and brown, star-strung night sky a brilliant midnight blue, somehow the same blue as Dominic's eyes just before he came inside her. The scent of the damp earth overpowered everything and even as she enjoyed walking in the night, exploring the forest like a child, Dominic seemed to be beside her, yet not visible the whole time.

The dreams were strange, yet so homey and comforting Mary had never slept so well in her whole life.

Chapter Ten

Dominic slowly, reluctantly felt himself waking up. He had been having the most magnificent dream. Thrusting in and out of his dream woman—Mary. She smelled so wonderful, tasted divine. Yet something was odd.

Frowning, keeping his eyes firmly shut, he desperately tried to stay in the dream.

Redhead. Luscious breasts. Delightful ass. *Sensitizing liquid.*

His eyes snapped open to stare at the darkened ceiling.

It hadn't been a dream. Mary had found him at the bar, after the gig with Sam and Lee. She had come home with him. He had fucked her thoroughly and she had practically fainted from sexual exhaustion.

He tried to turn onto his side to spoon her warm body closer to his and maybe start their antics once more.

Oh shit.

While from the waist down he turned onto his side. Something disturbingly familiar held his arms tied upright.

Craning his neck he looked up and saw the gag fluorescent pink fluffy handcuffs.

Well damn. His little Mary had been snooping while he slept.

Dominic grinned, wondering what to expect. Even though it was still night, the faint light outside his bedroom window showed it was only a few hours before dawn. He could hear water running down the sink in the bathroom, so he knew where Mary was. Fidgeting, he got himself comfortable, eagerly awaiting Mary's return.

After a few minutes, his patience was rewarded. The water turned off, and after a very brief pause the connecting door opened. His hungry gaze fell on the breathtaking sight of a naked Mary.

He felt his mouth water again.

She still looked as deliciously rounded as he remembered. Still as sexy and edible. He impatiently tugged on the cuffs, wondering if he should give away the secret. They had a catch in them that, if one knew where to flick, would unsnap the cuffs right away.

When Mary paused, ran a heated glance over his naked, and now fully aroused body, he decided to let her play with him a little longer. There was a far higher chance of them *both* enjoying themselves that way.

"Like what you see, love?"

"Oooh yeah. I can't wait to play with you. Tell me, do you really like chocolate mousse?"

Dominic frowned for a moment, and then remembered the huge dish of chocolate mousse Josephine had given him before he left the main house mid-afternoon Saturday.

"Oh. You found that. My sister-in-law gave it to me. Don't worry if you've eaten some for breakfast. There's enough to feed an army. I enjoy chocolate, but she and William are always making up huge batches of the stuff. They seem to have this private thing for chocolate."

"Oh no. I haven't eaten any. Yet."

With that, she walked out of the room. Dominic cocked his head to one side, to better hear her footsteps. When he heard her soft feet padding over into the small kitchen, and then the fridge door open, he knew what she was doing.

Hell, who was he to argue if a woman wanted to tie him up and feed him spoonfuls of chocolate mousse for breakfast? He didn't need to be home until later tonight. An al fresco breakfast with this immensely sexy woman would be the perfect way to start the morning.

He frowned at the thought of returning home without Mary. He felt sincerely attached to her, didn't feel his usual itchiness to shed her once the sun rose. Maybe he could convince her to come back with him, meet his siblings. If she had so many questions about him and his status as a werewolf, what better way to teach her than bring her home with him?

Still thinking through his options, he only half paid attention as Mary sat on the bed, cradling the huge bowl of mousse between her legs.

"You ready to answer some questions, big boy?"

Snapping back from his fantasies, he smiled teasingly up at her. "Sure thing, baby. Fire away."

"Okay. First up, is there much truth to those old '40s and '50s movies about werewolves? Do you turn into some slobbering, raving lunatic who eats fair maidens?"

Dominic laughed. He couldn't help it. Finally calming down, he managed to answer.

"Uh, no. While I don't think exactly the same as I do in human form, I am fully aware of everything I do, and retain pretty much full control of myself. I might get sidetracked by interesting scents, or chase some rabbits or squirrels, but I don't turn into a raving lunatic."

Mary nodded. She seemed as if she had already reached that conclusion for herself, which made him feel much happier.

"Does it hurt?"

Dominic frowned. "Does what hurt?"

"Changing, from a man to a wolf."

Dominic thought for a moment. "Not in a painful way, no. It's like…re-forming…returning back home…both ways. When I change into a wolf, I feel free, I sense so much more. Yet when I change back into human form, I feel…larger, smarter. It's hard to describe. It's as if I exist in both states semi-permanently. Both states offer me something different. We, my brothers and I, were raised to embrace both our selves. The animalistic side, who loves to hunt and run free, but also to enjoy our thinking, feeling human forms. How can it possibly hurt to return to one aspect of yourself?"

Mary nodded, her eyes far away, seeing something else.

"That must be so very nice. No wonder you can't settle down. I don't think I could either, given that opportunity. Oh, before you twist a finger trying to unsnap those handcuffs, I really ought to warn you I've taped them shut with some electrical tape. The release latch on the side won't work."

Dominic felt his eyes widen with shock. He was really stuck in these damn things?

Twisting his head back uncomfortably, he just barely saw a dark stretch of sticky black electrical tape. *Well damn!* "How the hell did you know to do that?"

Mary shrugged.

"Chloe, my other cousin, studied lock picking a few years back. She bought a trick set of handcuffs, teaching herself to get out of them. I learned a few things myself. Plus, I didn't really think you were the sort to have a *real* pair of handcuffs. Any set you had bought would obviously have a quick release."

Shuffling herself closer, Dominic eyed her warily.

"What are you doing?"

"Well first, I'm going to tie down your legs, so you don't think to kick me."

Dominic watched her tie his legs spread out to the footboard.

"Why would I want to kick you?"

"Patience, darling. You'll see soon enough."

When she had securely tied his legs to the footboard, she took a third satin strip and tied a rather large bow around his painfully erect shaft. Dominic didn't say anything—he merely raised an eyebrow. After surveying her work and nodding her satisfaction, she bent down and picked up the large bowl of mousse from the floor.

Dominic eyed the mousse. "Tell me you're going to feed it to me."

Mary merely grinned. Offering him a spoonful, he took it into his mouth, enjoying the light, fluffy chocolate melting on his tongue.

"Are you hungry? Or can you wait a while before I finish feeding you?"

Dominic's eyes rested on her full breasts.

"I think I have a different sort of hunger altogether."

Mary grinned. "Fantastic. Same here."

Carefully placing the heavy bowl next to his prone stomach, she straddled his hips. Dipping one finger into the nearly full bowl, she began to smear the mousse onto his stomach and abs.

Lifting his head, Dominic tried to see what she was drawing.

After a moment, Mary stopped. "Very pretty."

"You've just drawn your initials on me?"

Mary smiled.

"MD, what makes you think I haven't bestowed a Doctorate of Sex on you?"

"You've given a Doctorate of Sex to my *stomach*? Woman, evidently you've received the wrong impression about me. Maybe I need to be released and teach you a few more important things about myself."

Mary laughed and carefully placed the heavy bowl on the floor. Climbing back up onto the bed, she sat herself between Dominic's legs.

It was a strange feeling for him. Usually he took control

of the sexual games. Almost always *he* was between the legs of a pretty lady, not the other way around. The reversal of roles made his cock harden even more. It was a strange feeling. Strange, but wonderful.

Deciding to enjoy this time, he relaxed back into the soft bed and comfortable pillows.

"So, little Mary, you're going to cover me with chocolate mousse and let it dry all sticky? We could shower together, I know a few good moves in the shower."

"I'm sure you do, stud. But it would be an incredible waste of such a lovely mousse to let you do that. Anyway, this is *my* turn. My turn for control and to initiate the fun. I don't think you've quite learned to share."

Dominic smiled, a wide, toothy grin. "Ah, darling, trust me. You can take your turn and have all the control you want. Just as long as you make it worth my while."

Mary crept forward, her breasts and stomach pressing intimately against his iron-hard shaft. Oh-so-very-slowly, she stuck her tongue out and swiped a small amount of mousse from his abdomen.

Taking a lick of dessert into her mouth, she moaned softly. Dominic felt his mouth dry. Since when had chocolate mousse been the ultimate sexual toy and aphrodisiac? In that instant, he knew *exactly* what William and Josephine did with all that mousse they made.

Dominic swallowed, tried to get some moisture in his mouth. With that simple lick, Mary had bound him to her with chains of steel. He *needed* her now, craved her with a fire in his blood.

"Uh…Mary, love…"

Mary totally ignored him, too keen to have another taste of the mousse on his stomach.

As she took another lick into her delicate mouth, she sat back up, eyes closed, blissfully rolling the mousse around in her mouth.

"Did you know…" she started, swallowed, and then opened her eyes. "Did you know, those deliciously flat abdominal muscles of yours make the perfect table for chocolate mousse?"

Dominic suppressed a whimper of need. His cock was about to burst. Considering the number of times he had come, both inside and outside this beautiful woman in the last eight hours or so, he found it scary and marvelous that he *still* needed to come with the desperation and intensity of a man who had abstained for *years*.

"Uh…" he cleared his throat, unable to form a coherent thought.

"Don't worry," Mary grinned down at him, her nipples only just out of reach. If his hands were free he could…Dominic firmly brought his mind away from the multitude of things he would do if his hands were free.

When he felt Mary's tongue on his stomach again, he couldn't help himself. His hips rose by themselves and he thrust his body up, desperately begging her to do more.

"Down boy," she chided laughingly. "Impatient men only get teased longer with me. And don't pout or do that sad-puppy-dog-eyes thing with me either. That won't work."

Dominic laughed and shut his eyes. His body craved release, craved being lodged inside her to the hilt. Intuitively, he knew the more he pleaded and begged, the longer Mary would draw this out. Not that he could fake disinterest. His breath caught with every smooth-rough sweep of her tongue on his skin. His cock had begun to leak pre-cum. Each muscle in his stomach and legs twitched with excitement and repressed energy with every gentle caress of her hair and skin.

Nope. He didn't think he had a chance in hell of convincing her he wasn't fully focused and interested in what she was doing.

When the underside of Mary's soft chin bumped the fully

aroused and blood-bloated head of his shaft, electric currents jolted though him, made him moan and cry out.

When Mary merely winked at him, kissed the swollen head better, and returned to her torturous licking of the mousse, he fell back into the pillows with a cry.

He was in serious trouble.

Chapter Eleven

❧

Mary felt the light, fluffy chocolate melt inside her mouth. Now this was heaven. A delicious stud—both literally and figuratively—laid out in front of her, totally at her mercy.

Wet dreams were made out of scenarios just like this.

As she finished the last of the mousse, and continued to lick the last remains of the chocolate dessert from his body, she seriously considered what to do.

Initially, she had planned to get dressed and leave when she woke up. She didn't want to hang around for the inevitable "It's-been-fun-but-let's-call-it-a-day-I'll-give-you-a-call" conversation. Certainly, Dominic would be well versed in that particular speech, yet even though she knew it was coming, she still didn't want to hear it from his lips.

She wasn't stupid. She knew it was one night of mind-blowing, absolutely fantastic sex. Yet deep inside, in a place she would never admit to, Dominic had touched her. He wasn't some selfish, arrogant stud, who fucked for his own pleasure and not that of his partner.

He was a caring, sharing man who delighted in bringing pleasure to his partner. The fact that he was a Class A fuck merely made it that much better. Reality, however, was her small office and home back across the state. This sexual odyssey was more fantasy than reality. Very soon she would have to leave, before the polite but detached "It's been fun" lecture came around.

Feeling sad, yet relieved at the same time, Mary continued licking Dominic's now-sensitive skin. She clung to that relieved feeling. If they had decided on two nights, Sunday as well as Saturday, then she might have been fool enough to fall in love with the hunk.

She had no intention of joining the ranks of millions to give her heart to this man only to have it broken. Knowing Dominic as she now did, she knew he would never intentionally hurt a woman, but as her mother used to say, "hurt is hurt", whether it was intentional or not.

Thrusting the somber thoughts aside—there would be plenty of time to wallow in self-pity when she got back home—Mary lightly traced her hands back up his chest. Reaching his nipples, her destination, she lightly flicked them.

"Oh shit, love. Do that again," he moaned.

As requested, Mary toyed with his sensitive nipples as she nibbled and licked her way over his stomach, abs and up his chest.

Rubbing her lightly furred pussy over his straining erection, she gently kissed his mouth, relished the so-soft lips she was coming to crave.

Suddenly unsure whether to ask for what she was about to take, Mary gently continued to kiss him as she thought.

Should one ask a bound man for sex? Or simply take? What the hell is the etiquette in this sort of situation?

Thankfully, before she could think herself in circles, Dominic solved the problem for her.

"Shit, love. You're killing me. If you don't fuck me *right* now then my cock is going to explode all over you and you'll have to start again."

Mary laughed. "You know," she started, breathlessly, "I was just wondering if I should ask, or simply take."

"You can't rape the willing, love. And let me assure you, I'm so willing I'm likely to burst the instant your sweet pussy closes around me."

Mary smiled, far too busy lifting herself up over his large frame to bother with a reply.

With one smooth motion, she thrust herself down on him,

sheathing him and giving herself the exquisite pleasure of feeling her walls stretched to the limit.

They both cried out.

Mary noticed Dominic clenching his fists in their cuffs, desperately controlling his breathing.

"Do…oh my, you feel wonderful…" Realizing talk was beyond her capabilities, Mary simply reached up, stretching them both into new positions, and she fumbled with the cuffs.

"Hurry, love. With you stretched over me like this I think I'm about to lose what little control I've kept."

With fingers that simply wouldn't do what she requested of them, Mary finally unwrapped the electrical tape, and flicked the quick release lever. With a *snap* the cuffs opened and fell down unnoticed behind the headboard. Mary turned carefully to reach his feet.

Released from his bondage, both hands and feet, Dominic turned into a true pagan. Wild, excited beyond belief, he became sexy and grumpy at the same time.

"You, woman, will pay for that later. Be grateful I don't chain you to my bed for a year's worth of servitude for that."

Mary laughed, as Dominic rolled her beneath him.

"Hey!" she protested, laughingly, "it's my turn to be on top! Why else would I have to chain you down?"

Dominic grinned sexily. Running his palms up and down her sides, palming her large breasts, with just a few strokes he catalogued her every asset all over again. Thrusting even deeper into her, she squirmed as the silky scarf tied around his cock stopped him from penetrating her as deeply as possible.

Cursing a blue streak, Dominic literally ripped the thin silk from himself and spread her legs wider as he lodged himself so deeply into her she moaned and arched her back. Craving him even more deeply, Mary tried to drag his ass closer to her, to thrust himself even more deeply as he set a quick, hard pace between them.

"You can be on top," he panted, "in maybe a year or two when I've fully sated myself in you."

Mary blinked. *A year or two?* Just a manner of speaking, she assured herself. There was absolutely no point in raising her hopes. This man was the classic bad boy, the love 'em and leave 'em king. He was just being horny.

They both groaned as Dominic's pace grew more frenzied, wilder, even more pagan. He thrust into her faster and faster, with an almost blurring speed that had Mary's head spinning. His thick cock sent spirals of friction and pleasure shooting through her, arching her back with the pleasure. Surely one could die from sex as delicious as this?

Just when she felt certain she would explode from the immense feelings building inside her, Dominic lifted one of her hips, rotating to let himself penetrate her deeper. With the new angle, his heavy, engorged cock rubbed her G-spot, and she screamed.

The electric currents of pleasure she had been feeling were intensified a thousand-fold. Somewhere deep inside her, something broke apart and she felt a huge rush of emotions flow over her body.

The orgasm hit her with a startling, slightly scary velocity, and somewhere in the very back of her mind, she registered that she was screaming really loudly.

Mixed in with all these glorious feelings was the sharp nip of teeth. Dominic had bitten her neck! She giggled when she remembered only vampires were supposed to bite screaming virgins on the neck.

Mary giggled breathlessly. The bite didn't sting exactly, but she could feel it there, even when Dominic merely laved it with his tongue. The strange way it stung without hurting made her wonder if, for the first time in more years than she could count, she would have a hickey-like bruise when she woke up in the morning.

She frowned at the time he was taking over the bite.

Throughout the whole, he continued thrusting wildly inside her, claiming her with his cock as well as his mouth.

"Rabies shots up to date?" she panted.

"Don't get rabies, or any other human disease," he returned, just as breathless.

Mary nodded, and let the immense feelings wash over her.

Before she could think or question any further, Dominic was coming. Shooting hot loads of his seed deep in her body, he shuddered and pulled her so closely into his body she felt as if parts of them merged into the other.

Hugging him back, just as tightly, she relished the feeling of her sweaty body pressed deeply into his sweaty body.

Finally, he collapsed onto her, panting, his muscles shaking slightly. She curled up into his body, enjoying the heat, and that special closeness one always experiences after a particularly wonderful bout of sex.

As the minutes ticked by, her body cooled, and she shivered. Dominic groaned a little, sat up and pulled the coverlet up to cover them both. He then settled back as close to her body he could possibly be, and still be able to breathe.

He held her firmly, keeping her in place beside him, one arm around her back, pulling her breasts flush against his chest, the other arm possessively cupping her ass.

His legs tangled around hers making sure that practically every point along their bodies touched, skin on skin. Smiling down at her face, he drew her closer into the circle of his arms as he sleepily closed his eyes, a sated look on his face.

"We needta talk..." he murmured.

Mary felt a shaft of pain go through her. Suddenly wide-awake, she hoped to placate him. Obviously on the verge of sleep, she decided to soothe him, hoping he would fall asleep, not talk. Stroking his cheek softly, she reached up to switch off the bedside lamp.

"That's okay, Dom. I understand. Just go to sleep, I can pack and go later."

"No…" he huskily protested. "Too tired now. Explain later. Want you to stay."

"Shhh…just sleep now."

Dominic continued murmuring, but it was the drowsy, half-asleep nonsense of a small child as it fights off sleep. Mary had been feeling pretty damn tired herself after such an explosive climax. Yet now she simply wanted to start the long trek home.

She didn't think she could make the ten-hour trip after so little sleep and such a long night and day, but she could certainly get an hour or two's worth of driving in and crash at a motel before finishing the journey.

Indulging herself, she stroked Dominic's cheek for a few more minutes, until she was certain he was fully asleep, still murmuring nonsense. She enjoyed every second of the safe feeling lying cradled in his arms gave her. She enjoyed feeling the heat radiate from his body, and the subtle yet completely masculine possessiveness of his muscled legs pressed between her own, claiming her even while he slept.

Mary braced herself, assuring herself once more he was fully and deeply asleep, and climbed slowly, carefully from the giant bed.

The chilly morning air brought her back to her senses and helped wake her up a little. Scampering around the small apartment, she found her clothes and dressed without the light. There was a lightening of the sky, showing dawn did indeed draw closer, even when one didn't want it to.

Mentally checking each item she had arrived with, she crossed over to the desk. Scrambling around in the near dark, she wrote a brief, succinct note.

Thank you for an unbelievable night. I didn't want to hang around for the morning-after speech. Hope you don't mind. You will always be in my thoughts, and I will remember you whenever I hear

Night Prowler. *Mary.*

Refusing to feel either guilt for leaving the cowardly way, or a pang at the thought of never sharing such mind-blowing sex with this man again, Mary picked up her purse and left the apartment.

Chapter Twelve
Early Wednesday morning

જી

"*Dominic*! I swear if you don't stop pacing I'm gonna have to get up and pound you! You're giving me a headache."

Dominic ignored his brother and continued to pace in front of the huge windows overlooking the large house's backyard. The kids were all playing a mixture of Chase, and Hide and Seek, depending on who was winning.

"How can I be giving you a headache when you're supposed to be updating the latest security measures?"

"Rather easily, bro. You're a large presence, remember? With you stalking back and forth like a caged wolf it's quite hard to miss you. Why don't you just admit you love the girl and go mate with her? I thought you were this legendary seducer—so go seduce her and convince her to marry you."

Dominic ran a hand through his shoulder-length hair, mussing it further. "It's not that easy."

"Really. Why not?"

Dominic resumed his pacing. "She only wanted to find out about my werewolf side. I was a novelty. She was curious. We both got our questions answered and some unspeakably good sex. End of story."

Samuel leaned back in his chair, a huge grin on his face.

"Oh, how the mighty have fallen. So unspeakably good sex is no longer enough?"

"No, damn you! It's not enough. Not for one night."

Samuel leaned forward, a devilish gleam in his eye.

"Wow, bro. If the sex is really that good, maybe I

should—"

"Don't you *dare*!"

Dominic paused, realized his beloved brother had set him up and caught him like some gauche youth.

"Har-har. Very funny. Fine, I love the girl. Happy?"

Throwing himself into the over-padded armchair, he pouted as Samuel clutched his heart as if he were having an attack.

"Oh, the shock! The surprise! You love the girl. Finally! How long did it take you to admit it?"

"This isn't funny, Sam."

Sighing, Dominic ran a hand through his already messy hair and idly scratched his two days worth of stubble. Samuel typed in a few keystrokes, only half paying attention. He knew in a moment or two...

"Well...what the hell do *you* think I should do, seeing as you're so smug about the whole thing?" Dominic grumpily asked, obviously hating the fact he needed help in this of all areas.

Samuel looked at him as if he had lost his mind. "Why, little brother, I do believe you should chase after her, get down on your knees, and beg for her to stay with you."

Dominic raised one eyebrow arrogantly.

Samuel shrugged. "Or seduce her senseless and wring promises out of her, then bully her to keep them until she's fool enough to love you in return."

Dominic stared out the window, mulling over his choices, his brain ticking away for the first time since he had woken up, cold and alone in his large bed.

"You still okay with me offering the kid a summer job in the company?"

"Sure! Anyone good enough to crack your code is welcome to come work for us. We can use kids that skilled."

Dominic nodded. "I might start with that. At least I'll have some balm to soothe my pride if she turns me down flat."

"You're sure she's the 'One'?"

Dominic turned to his brother, hearing him uncertain for the first time in what felt like years.

"Yeah. I'm sure. I marked her, I dream of her, *crave* her worse than any sort of drug. I can't really explain it. I feel like there's this piece missing out of me. I've been in a shitty mood since she left—"

Samuel rolled his eyes comically.

"You don't say! Sounds to me more like a case of the flu than true love. You can count me out on love if this is the sort of moron it produces!"

Dominic swiped him, catching him on the shoulder.

"Enough outta *you*! You realize you're next! With the rest of us mated, you have no hope. Soph and Josie will be focusing on you. You, my dearest brother, are as good as mated! I can't wait to give *you* love advice! Hopefully it'll be a spitfire just like my Mary, and *then* we'll see who's such a hopeless case."

Samuel scoffed.

"No way, man. With Art and Wills reproducing like rabbits, and you won't be so far behind, there's no need for me to mate. I think I'll stay the happy bachelor uncle. Art and Wills are touched in the head now that they're getting regular spectacular sex and have a ton of kids to look out for. Christiana will start dating soon enough. *Woo-whee*, I can't wait to see how Art will react to *that*! I'm perfectly happy to sit back and watch."

Dominic merely smiled. "Sure, Sam. Whatever. I should probably tape this with one of your gadgets and have it replayed nightly once you fall like a ton of bricks. It really isn't so bad once you get used to it."

With that, he stood up and stretched, happy for the first

time all week.

"In fact, it feels quite refreshing. I don't feel this insane urge to fuck every sexy woman I meet, anymore. I don't feel like going out and picking anyone up. I just want my Mary. I might head out. The sooner I get this over with, the happier I'll be."

Samuel rose and hugged his brother.

"Just make sure you shower and shave first, girls like that sort of thing apparently. Man, you're a goner, Dom. Remember what I said about your knees and begging. If your famous seduction technique doesn't work, then think of that silver tongue of yours and how much women like men to be on their knees groveling."

Dominic tried to get him in a headlock. The brothers scuffled for a few moments, bumping into chairs, knocking a lamp over. They were both so involved in getting one up on the other they didn't hear the door open until a young high-pitched voice cried out.

"Mom! Uncle Dom and Uncle Sam are fighting in Dad's study again! They've knocked over the lamp you gave him, too! They need a time-out!"

Both men hastily unlocked themselves and glared fiercely at Edward and Christiana, who stared at them from the doorway as if they were a pair of naughty six-year-olds.

Christiana waggled her finger, a perfect imitation of Sophie when she was riled.

"Fighting is to remain outside. You'll put holes in the rugs and walls again. You know the rules!"

Edward looked at the men, surprisingly mature for his seven years. Christiana, only four, enjoyed the thought of her mom chastising her huge uncles.

"Don't be a tattletale, Christi," Edward chastised quietly.

Christiana pouted. "But—"

Edward continued as if she hadn't even interrupted, sure

in that way only kids have, that his words would be heeded. "They were only playing. And anyway, Dominic is going to go get his mate. Aren't you?"

Surprised by the astuteness of the young lad, Dominic nodded solemnly.

"Sure am, Edward. Now if you'll excuse me, I need to go pack before your Aunt Sophie comes to read me a lecture and lock me in my bedroom for an hour of time-out."

Christiana turned to Edward.

"How could Mom *read* him a lecture? She just waggles her finger and talks lots."

"Come on, hotshot. I'll tell you out back."

Samuel laughed as Edward dragged Christiana out into the backyard, and began to talk quickly to her. The men found it amusing that she hung on his every word.

As they quickly left the study, they noticed Zachariah staring after the two kids, a proud, happy look in his eyes.

"You okay, Grandpa?"

Zachariah snapped back to reality. "Sure am, Dom. I hear you're off to pick up your mate? Congratulations, son."

Dominic rolled his eyes. "It's not a done deal, Gramps. She's gotta accept me first."

Zachariah snorted. "The day one of you men can't twist a decent female around your left paw is the day I take you out back and thump your hide raw! You've had the ladies drooling over you since before you were a teen. I'm sure you'll manage."

The old man turned to Samuel. "And you had better look out for yourself, my boy. You think you won't settle down. Let me warn you, lad. You're gonna meet her right when you don't want to, don't expect to, and she'll lead you a merry dance, just like all the other boys. So don't get too cocky, you hear?"

Samuel merely grinned. "Me? Cocky? Grandpa, I'm

shattered!"

The old man snorted, and turned around muttering. "Damned youth of today. No idea! No respect!"

The two men laughed, certain that their grandfather had a large grin across his features. They headed out the back, Dominic plotting how to tame his redhead.

* * * * *

Later Wednesday afternoon

"*Mary*! Please stop that pacing, you're giving me the most horrendous headache."

Mary ignored her cousin and continued to pace in front of her office window. "How can I possibly be giving you a headache when you're supposed to be practicing your touch typing?"

"Rather easily, hon. With you swinging back and forth like a pendulum behind the monitor, I'm beginning to feel seasick!"

Mary stopped pacing to stare out the window into her small green backyard. With a squeak of the chair, Chloe stood up and came over to her cousin.

"Why don't you go back, hon? It's obvious you've left stuff undone with Dominic."

Mary shook her head.

"He's a one-night stand man. There's no way he wants a meaningful relationship, and there's no way at this stage I'd settle for anything less."

Chloe rolled her eyes. "You convinced him to have a one-night stand, why not seduce him into an affair? From there you can move into a relationship."

Mary shook her head. "He's not like that. He's a love 'em and leave 'em man. I'd just end up getting hurt."

"Sure," Chloe scoffed, "and like you're not hurt now."

Mary pressed her lips together. She *was* hurt, but it was so much more than that.

Through the past three nights since she'd been with Dominic, she had been dreaming the most erotic dreams. Far more heated and desperate than any other erotic night journey in the past.

She woke each morning, the small hickey he had given her throbbing with a desperate need that pounded just as demandingly in her pussy.

She had already worn out two sets of vibrator batteries. Nothing seemed to compare with her Dominic, and she was getting worried. How could a girl get over a one-night stand, when one relived each and every moment nightly? When one's dreams *added* the fantasies to one's memory?

"I think I need to go shopping. Want to come watch me splurge on a new pair of shoes?"

Chloe sighed and went to shut off the computer. "Why not? Matthew is still reading that new coding book, isn't he? He'll be fine for a few more hours at least. We might as well pick up the makings for dinner, too. How that boy manages to eat twice as much as the two of us combined is beyond me."

Mary hugged her cousin. "We can check on him on the way out. And apparently growing young men eat like crazy. Next thing we'll know he'll be not only taller than us, but bigger and stronger. The days when we could scold him and tower over him telling him he was to do what we said are unfortunately long gone. We should have enjoyed them more when we had them."

"I hear you, sweetie. Let's go spend some money. I have the latest Victoria's Secret catalogue in my bag somewhere..."

Mary laughed as she and Chloe left her small study. Nothing like spending a bundle of money on sexy lingerie, shoes and tops to cheer a girl up.

Arm-in-arm, the cousins went in search of their young man, and to soothe themselves with an afternoon of shopping.

Chapter Thirteen

℘

Dominic studied the small but neatly kept front garden. A great expanse of neatly trimmed grass had some surrounding flowers and foliage, but still retained its simplicity and overall green feeling.

Double-checking the address he had copied from his files before leaving, he made sure he wasn't about to scare some innocent stranger. He wasn't sure what his infamous plan was, but he knew something would come to him. It always did.

He switched off the ignition of his large motorcycle and removed his helmet. Shaking out his sweaty hair, he let the wind blow through it for a moment. He had made the long drive in record time. Looking at the almost-set sun, he cringed slightly as he prayed silently in grateful gratitude to have not racked up speeding fines along the long highways.

Removing his leather gloves, he ran his hands through his shoulder-length waves in the futile attempt to bring some order to his locks.

Deciding nothing earth-shattering would come to him procrastinating outside Mary's home, he climbed off the huge machine. Just like him, it was dark, powerful and full of thrust.

Grinning at the wicked thought, he stalked up the front path. Passing the neatly weeded flowers, he smiled at the similar wildflowers growing haphazardly as were in his own backyard. He liked the garden. It was neat, yet unrestrained. Much like his Mary.

Ringing the doorbell, thoughts of what he could do to Mary as she opened the door flitted through his mind. Foremost in his fantasies was backing her up against the wall and kissing her senseless. A very close second was ripping her clothes off, tearing off his own, and plunging balls deep into her without any preliminaries or words.

With a large grin on his face, he felt his cock lengthen and become painfully erect beneath his leather pants as he heard light footfalls coming down the hall towards the closed door.

He felt an incredible spurt of disappointment as a tall, lanky teenage boy opened the door, looking vaguely suspicious.

"Who the hell are you?" he demanded rudely.

"You must be Matthew Dennison. I'm a friend of your cousin Mary."

Much of the hostility seeped out of the boy, but the wariness and caution remained.

"She's not home. I can leave her a message that you dropped by. What's your name?"

Dominic grinned. "Oh, I'll stick around. You and I have a few things to talk about."

Some of the teen's hostility returned. "Talk about? Huh?"

Dominic leaned forwards, slightly intimidating. It wouldn't do to really scare the kid. Mary would be pissed if he did that. But intimidating him a little wouldn't hurt, particularly seeing as like most teenagers he seemed to talk in monosyllables. If the kid were to grow up with a decent job, he might as well start learning now.

"It's polite and hospitable to let a guest enter one's home when they have business to discuss."

Matthew bit his lip as he obviously contemplated the wisdom of letting him in.

"Business?" he questioned, more politely than he so far had acted.

Dominic nodded. "A little matter from Rutledge Security Company. My name is Dominic Rutledge."

The boy whitened considerably. Dominic cursed himself.

He hadn't truly meant to scare the kid, just shake a bit of the cockiness out of him.

"Mary had nothing to do with that! It was just me! You can't touch her on that!"

Dominic sighed. "Look, Matthew. The thing is, I know it was you, and your cousin merely got you untangled. I've talked to my brothers and we want to offer you a traineeship on strict conditions. You're skilled. You know you are, and we want to drag you onto the straight and narrow, away from your idiot friends. Can we chat about this inside, or do you want your nosy next-door neighbor—who is currently peering at us through the curtains, by the way—to listen to every word?"

The boy stepped aside to let him enter surprisingly quickly. Dominic entered, prepared to put forward his best spiel.

At least the kid didn't seem so hostile anymore, he had probably only been defensive of his cousin's home. That was a good thing, in Dominic's mind. Anyone prepared to care for and protect his Mary gained points in his estimation.

* * * * *

Mary let herself and Chloe into her house, pleased and surprised when they entered to the smell of meat simmering. She sniffed. Smelled a little like tacos. The large black motorcycle parked outside their house, on the other hand, had her worried. If one of Matthew's dropkick friends had stopped by to dare him into something else illegal and stupid she'd have a hissy fit.

"Matthew?"

"In here, Mar. We're cooking dinner."

Mary blinked, her heart sinking. *We?* Not good, not good at all.

Chloe picked up on it too. "Matthew Dennison, you

better not have invited a horde of your friends over for dinner. Mary and I have just spent a fortune on shoes and girls' stuff and can't afford to feed your mass of thousands!"

"Oh no! Oof—"

Mary sighed and set down her two shoeboxes, three shopping bags crammed full of naughty Victoria's Secret gear, and two new low-cut tops on the side table. She had better find out whom Matthew was entertaining.

"I've had a rough day, Matthew. I swear if you're in trouble again—"

Mary felt her throat tighten and her head go light as she entered her kitchen to find Dominic in black leathers standing over her stove in her grandmother's white frilled apron stirring meat and tomatoes.

He took a quick look over his shoulder, grinned boldly at her and continued to stir the simmering mixture.

"Matt, can you please continue slicing the lettuce and tomato and grating the cheese? We wanted this done by the time your family arrived home, right?"

"Sure thing, Dominic. So you're sure your brothers aren't pissed at me for that hacking stunt?"

"Language, boy!" Mary choked out, still trying to believe what her eyes were showing her. Dominic was happy to wear a white ancient frilly *apron*?

"Yeah, watch those words, sport. And yeah, they were…upset. But once we realized we could use your skills to test the holes in our security, and use your youth and…uh…enthusiasm, they were happy to bring you on board. But like I said, there are strict conditions. Any brushes with the law, for *anything*, means we review not only your work with us, but also that whole pressing charges issue. You'll also need to be honest and up front with us. Anyone offering you money or asking you to do dodgy stuff you need to come to us straight away. We don't hire and keep on people we don't trust."

"Sure, man. I can deal with that. So you'd, like, teach me shi...uh... stuff? Like more complex coding and firewalls and stuff?"

"Sure will. You can teach us stuff too, like where you found our holes, and how you go about doing that without setting off the alarms. It'll be the normal give-and-take."

"Neat! Can I tell my friends what I'm doing?"

"In part, you obviously can't give them details of the systems we show you, but you can tell them that you're working for us and helping us beef up and constantly upgrade our security measures. That should be enough to impress your buddies."

"Way cool!"

"Um. Excuse this feminine interruption, but what the hell is going on?"

Dominic frowned at her, a grin tugging at the corner of his mouth. "Language, Mary! What will the boy think?"

Mary crossed her arms over her chest and started tapping a foot, clearly picturing in her mind strangling Dominic. He might look like sex and sin in black leather and her apron, but that wouldn't excuse him for butting into her cousin's life.

"I'm offering Matthew a decent job. You did say he was starting college next term and was looking for interim work to keep himself out of mischief." He ignored the cry of protest from Matthew at his declaration. "Samuel and I talked about his obvious skill and decided to use him as an asset to the company. Art and Wills agreed."

"Yeah," Matthew interjected, "and then Dominic suggested we start dinner for you and Chloe, 'cos we weren't sure when you'd get back and we were getting hungry."

Mary rolled her eyes. Obviously he had a conquest in Matthew. She wondered what his plans for her were. Remembering his hospitality with her, she decided she might as well seal the deal.

"Do you have a place to stay?"

Gleaming blue eyes looked back at her. Wicked mischief and a very faint wariness lay within the deep blueness of his eyes. As if he were scared of her rejection, but determined all the same.

"No."

She nodded, resigned. "You can bunk here in the spare room. Chloe and Matthew live close by but will stay for dinner. I'm having a shower."

Hoping he caught the warning and faint promise she had delivered him, she stalked out of the room without looking back. Earlier in the day she'd have given anything to have him here. Now she wasn't so sure.

What the hell would she do if he was only here for another single night, before taking Matthew back with him? Closing the door to her bedroom firmly shut, she started stripping as she headed into her bathroom. Turning the water on very hot and strong, she stepped into the shower and let the hot spray pour down on her.

There was no point in worrying and fretting. She would find out what Dominic wanted soon enough.

Chapter Fourteen

ಐ

Dominic mentally congratulated himself. After cleaning and putting away all the dishes they had used, Matthew finally dragged Chloe back home to tell her all about his new job. Now he finally had Mary all to himself.

As she sat in her exceedingly comfortable recliner, sipping on her mug of Earl Grey tea, she nervously gazed at him over the rim of her cup. He grinned, a happy, possessive, truly wolfish grin.

She quickly lowered her eyes and returned to sipping her hot tea. Dominic perched on the edge of the couch, content to wait her out. They both knew there was unfinished business between them, and for the moment, Dominic allowed Mary to stall him.

"So you're really offering him work until the term starts?"

"Sure am. If the little joker is good enough to get into the system, Sam and I think he could be an asset. Artemais and William are prepared to trust us. If he wants, and can help us out, Matthew is even welcome to stay on part-time while at college. It's up to him and what he can do for us. Either way, it will certainly keep him out of trouble for a while."

Dominic stared at his love. She boldly stared back at him, stiffening her spine.

"I don't want an affair with you," she stated, setting the mug down on the small table. She rose and started to pace. Dominic grinned.

He hadn't know she paced when anxious or thinking heavily. Same as him. The knowledge made him happier than he'd been all week, since awakening to that damned note and a cold, empty bed.

"Who said anything of an affair, Mary love?"

"I don't want another freakin' one-night stand either! What the hell do you call a two-night stand? How juvenile and stupid does that sound? Two-night stand indeed!"

Dominic struggled to keep a straight face. "What *do* you want, Mary?"

She whirled on him, her hair flying out of its ponytail, green eyes snapping angrily. She was so small, the fact she was certain she could take him on made him want to laugh. At five-foot-two, she was pretty damn short when compared to him. Even so, the innate knowledge inside her that he would never hurt her made him relieved.

She stormed up to him, so he kept still, not wanting to interrupt her. She came right up to his chest, so her nipples nearly brushed his shirt. She poked him, angrily punctuating her words.

"You want to know what I want? I want you to stay with me. I want you to go to sleep curled next to me every night and wake up next to me every morning. I want you to *commit* to me. I know you have no concept of the word, but it's a nice one—you can get used to it. No more floozies, no more indiscriminate fucking. Just us."

She paused, her eyes widening slightly with the shock of what she had just said. Immediately, she started to back away.

Dominic reached out and grabbed the wrist of the hand that had been poking him.

"I can deal with that, as long as the conditions are the same for you. If you expect faithfulness from me, I demand the same in return. Tit-for-tat after all, Mary love."

If anything, her eyes widened more. He had surprised her. He found he liked the warmth that stole through him, making him desperately want to laugh.

"You'd do that? You'd commit to me. I'm not talking for a

short time, Dom. I'm taking long-term here."

Dominic reached into the pocket of his pants, withdrew a small velvet box. Holding it out, he offered it to Mary.

She looked from it to him and back again, her mouth open and her eyes wide. He felt like laughing and puking from nerves at the same time. She wasn't the only one surprised and off-kilter here.

Smiling mischievously, enjoying her shock and surprise if nothing else, he caught only a glimpse of the tear lodged in her sparkling eye.

"Aren't you supposed to be down on your knees, begging?" she asked huskily.

Dominic laughed outright. "Samuel warned me the ladies like to see men on their knees begging. For once, he was right."

He fell down to his knees, still holding one of her wrists. He looked up into the face that had captured his heart, into the eyes full of laughter and intelligence.

"Mary, love. Will you marry me?"

Her face split into a grin.

"What happened to flowers and music? I'm sure there's supposed to be candy and declarations of undying love." She sobered up for a moment. "I do love you, you know. Chloe can tell you I've been like a wounded bear the past few days."

Dominic smiled back at her. "Samuel could give you a similar accounting. I love you too. You should know that. What the hell else could get me down on my knees?"

Mary nodded. Dominic opened the box, showing her a gleaming emerald in a platinum setting. The emerald had the same fire and depth as her eyes. Mary thought it perfect.

Dominic slid it on her finger, a thrill of possession and happiness going through him. Rising quickly, he scooped her up into his arms.

"Hey! That begging thing didn't last long!" she laughed,

squashed against his chest.

Dominic nipped at her neck, muffling his laughter as he stalked through the room, down the hall, and into her small bedroom.

"You should have enjoyed it while it lasted. I can promise that won't be happening too often, love."

Mary laughed as he gently dropped her on the bed. Bouncing once, she rolled onto her back to look up at him. She watched him tug impatiently at his shirt.

"In a rush, darling?"

"To get naked, yes. To fuck you mindless, oh no. No, I think I'll take my time with that particular task. I need to relearn every inch of your skin, to re-lick every inch of you."

Mary kicked off her sneakers and started tugging at her jeans. "May I try to tempt you to change your mind?"

Dominic laughed as he began to unbuckle his jeans. "Mary, love. You can try to tempt me to anything. Just a warning, I intend to take my time this go-around. Maybe next time you can set the pace."

Dominic stepped out of his leather pants just as Mary cleared her jeans from her ankles. She tried to hold him off with her feet, but he simply dodged around them and crashed down onto her on the bed.

"Hey!" she protested, trying not to laugh, "I'm not naked yet!"

"Don't worry, love, I'll start down at your feet. We can work our way up."

"But my panties…"

"Are made of extra thin lace and won't pose even a minute barrier. Trust me."

"I do. Trust you, I mean."

Dominic looked deep into her eyes and kissed her hard. Pulling away with difficulty, he grinned down at her.

"Same here, love. But I am determined to do this slow. I've missed you the past few days. I need to make up that lost time. Starting with a foot massage."

Mary groaned, as he started to expertly massage her feet. Peppering kisses along her sole and ankle, he spiced up what would have been a fantastic massage anyway.

She laughed as he muttered where the different parts of her sole led to pulse points. As he pressed one side of the ball of her foot, massaging it and sending an electric current of pleasure through her, he would mutter "headaches" or "dizziness" and other tidbits of information.

Laughing, she finally pulled her foot from his grasp, and straddled him.

"My turn," she laughed.

Tearing his shirt from him, she watched with glee as his buttons popped from the shirt.

Bending down, she nibbled happily at his chest, licking and enjoying the taste of his skin. She shrieked when she was rolled underneath him again.

"No fair!" she cried out, trying hard not to start laughing again.

"My turn," he teased.

"But I hadn't finished!"

He pressed his lips against hers, sealing off her complaints. Touching her everywhere, Dominic enjoyed her body as he had longed to do these last few days. He ran his hands all over her, starting with her breasts, then moving to her hungry nipples down the smooth line of her torso down to her waist, and then her hips.

Mary panted, arching into his soft touch. When she spread her legs in wanton invitation, he simply couldn't resist.

Lodging himself just barely inside her, he looked into her eyes, lost himself in her heated gaze.

"This is forever," he warned her. He felt his heart

overflow with happiness as she merely smiled and canted her hips, nudging him further inside her heat. He thrust into her, feeling himself bathed in her heat, her love, in their mingled desire and hunger for each other.

Quickly, they both reached for that peak, that perfect moment only the best of lovers ever truly find. Crying out into each other's mouths, lost for breath or words, they collapsed together, sweaty and content.

Long into the night they touched and caressed, relearning and discovering each other. They both panted, screamed and groaned, the sheer ecstasy washing over them until they merged completely, totally as one over and over.

They whispered secret words, lover's words and promises. Dominic could barely believe how happy and sated he felt. He knew he would never again feel the melancholy dissolution he used to feel after his forgettable women. Eventually, they both fell asleep, entwined together, loving every moment they had spent in each other's embrace.

Epilogue
A few months later

∞

"So you have to add the chocolate chips in *after* you've mixed the cookie dough and only just before you throw them on the tray?"

"Sure do, otherwise you tend to eat more chocolate than you put into the dough."

Chloe nodded solemnly and continued to scribble down instructions.

"And you say that's enough cookie dough for twelve children—so a class of twenty thirteen-year-olds we should—what?—double it just to be safe?"

Mary fiddled nervously with her hem. Her stupid veil—which had been Chloe's damn idea, not hers anyway—was touching the roof of the tiny beat-up Ford Escort and was driving her nuts.

Sophie was driving Chloe's car, dressed in a casual, flirty summer dress. Chloe was sitting in the passenger seat, madly scrawling notes on a napkin she had found among the mess in the glove box.

Mary smiled and looked outside the window. She felt like throwing up, again, and refused to give in to her nerves.

Chloe continued to grill Mary's soon-to-be sister-in-law on simple, effective recipes. She would be filling in for a friend's Home Economics class for a semester and needed quick, easy recipes to teach a bunch of overenthusiastic thirteen-year-olds.

After what felt like forever, they finally pulled into the small chapel. Nestled amongst the trees of the National Park, it was a tiny, rustic little thing.

It was beautiful.

Matthew paced out front, obviously as agitated as Mary felt. He would walk her down the aisle. Chloe came around to the back to help her get her enormous dress—had she *really* thought such a huge white wedding dress would be fun?— and veil out of the car still intact.

Finished with straightening her dress and veil, Chloe automatically moved her hand to push the now-crumpled note-ridden napkin in what would have been her jeans pocket. If she hadn't been wearing a short, brightly colored summery dress.

"Damn. Why couldn't I have worn my jeans, Mar? I'd be so much more comfortable in them."

"Bridesmaids *don't* wear jeans."

Chloe grumbled under her breath and pushed the napkin into the cup of her bra.

"If I ever get married, which I never will, remind me of how uncomfortable these damn shoes are and how much I hate dresses. I promise *you* can wear jeans to my wedding."

Mary laughed, forgetting for a moment how nauseous she felt. Surely the time for bridal jitters was over? When would her stomach settle down?

"Mar? Are you okay? You look like you're about to puke."

Mary vaguely felt Chloe place a worried hand to her forehead. "Mar? You okay?"

Swallowing down the nausea, she nodded.

"What is it? You can't possibly be having doubts?"

"No. I'm not, it's just my stomach."

Chloe crunched her head in thought. "Hey, when was your last period?"

Mary blinked. The dots in her mind connected, and she

felt a huge weight lift from her shoulders. Strange how Chloe was often one of the most perceptive people she knew. How could she have *not* worked something so simple out?

"Oh, man. He's going to flip. We've been trying for months now."

Matthew cleared his throat, obviously not wanting to butt in, but taking his duties rather seriously. He had become far more mature in the short time working for the Rutledges'. Both Mary and Chloe were happy but surprised at the changes in their little relative.

"Much as this is amusing and exciting, I really should point out Dominic is probably pacing a hole in the floor in there. Chloe, set up her skirts, or whatever it is you should do. Let's get moving."

Mary felt so relieved she was in a daze. As if floating on clouds, she completely ignored her slight nausea and followed her cousin into the foyer of the small chapel. Happily holding Matthew's arm, she smiled as the theme to *St. Elmo's Fire* started and with an enthusiastic wink and thumbs-up, Chloe began to tread down the aisle in front.

Mary tried not to snicker at the ginger way Chloe placed one foot solidly in front of the other. Except for her senior prom, she had never worn heels before, and even then she had removed her shoes on the dance floor.

Mary had warned her to practice in the new shoes, but if the waver in her ankles and tender way she placed each foot in front of the other, she'd bet money on her cousin not practicing at all.

Then again, Chloe had ducked out of all but two of her supposed "fittings", insisting only the bride needed to be in the form-fitting dress. It had taken bribes, threats, and finally tearful pleadings to get Chloe to fall in line. Even if the tears had been fake, Mary was glad they had worked. Chloe looked fantastic.

There were only a handful of guests, whom she smiled at

as she began to walk down the aisle with Matthew carefully counting the beats of the music under his breath.

Zachariah was seated between Christiana and Edward—both waving merrily and throwing rose petals already. Mary grinned at a few of her work buddies and extended family members she recognized.

The flowers decorating the pews were wild and gorgeous, Mary felt glad she had left the wildlife parts to Dom. The sun shone through the small stained glass windows, and made the whole setting surreal and perfect.

Mary frowned slightly when she noticed Chloe had paused in her progression down the aisle. She only halted a moment, and then jerkily moved forward to her place near the priest. Mary looked around, wondering what had upset her cousin.

Dominic stood right there, beaming his pride and love. Only the electric feelings emanating from Chloe made Mary continue to look. Samuel stood next to Dominic, standing up for him as Chloe stood up for her.

For just a moment, Mary wondered…then cast aside all thoughts of her cousin. Chloe could wait a day or two.

She smiled as Matthew placed a chaste kiss on her cheek, and handed her proudly over to Dominic. He bent over, and only because she stood so close to them, she overheard her young cousin whisper, "*Now* she's your problem—one down, one to go!" to her soon-to-be-husband.

Dominic grinned wickedly and winked.

Mary clutched her True Mate's hands—his words, not hers, but the label strangely seemed to suit them. As the priest spoke the words to unite them forever, she stared into eyes as deep and blue as the ocean. She could feel his pulse burning though his wrist, feel the simmering lust and energy inside his body, waiting to spring free and consume her.

She knew her eyes twinkled with the secret knowledge she held inside her. Dominic had insisted on having a large family. They were still cajoling and bribing each other on exactly how many children they wanted. Mary wanted three; Dominic insisted on eight.

With number one safely tucked away inside her, she was sure they could reach some mutually satisfying arrangement.

Mary looked into the eyes she would always come home to. She couldn't wait to get back to their cabin. She had a feeling this would be one night neither she nor Dominic would ever forget.

MY HEART'S PASSION

附

Prologue
Wednesday

જી

"Are you sure you and Dominic don't mind?"

Mary laughed huskily.

"Chloe darling, I'm still feeling like a newlywed, even after six months. The last place Dominic and I want is to be within spitting distance of his nieces, nephews, and siblings. They're a great bunch, and we certainly love them to bits, but someone is always dropping around, interrupting us at delicate moments to have a chat with us, or to play a game of Chase or something. We're only going away for four and a half days, and we're only renting a cabin thirty miles on the other side of the park — but trust me, no one is going to disturb us and we can have some fun before bub arrives and we *can't* make polite or even half-believable excuses anymore."

Chloe grinned. "One last fuck-fest before you become responsible adults, hmm?"

Mary laughed. "Who said anything about being responsible, Chlo? I'm only talking about having a baby — not starting a career in politics or something."

Chloe rolled her eyes and heard an answering snicker from the other end of the line. They might be on opposite sides of the state, but Chloe shared a special closeness with her cousin. They were best friends as well as family.

"Anyway," Mary continued, "I think you'll enjoy the break — after six months of standing in as a high school teacher anyone would need a break. Just don't complain to me when all the rugrats over here insist you play games with them. They're darling children — but they'll drive you nuts if you let them."

"I think I can handle a handful of overenthusiastic kids after subbing for six months and coping with thirty junior high teenagers in a cooking class. As long as the kids don't start a food fight, we'll get along just fine."

"A long weekend away, hopefully hidden in the cabin, might give you the time you need to think about where you want to go now."

Chloe sighed. "Mar, please don't start on that again. You know I don't want to study anymore."

Chloe's refusal to keep a steady job, what she liked to refer to as her "itchy feet" was a running joke between the two of them. She couldn't bear the thought of bogging herself down in more studies. Instead, she had taken the first available job after graduating high school.

Moving from job to job, Mary had shown constant astonishment at her innate skill to pick up jobs with ease, and then finding something different to do.

"Well, some time out in the cabin might be helpful to you. Take a break and you can think about things and read to your heart's content. I've already mailed you the keys, so we'll leave very early tomorrow morning. You can move in anytime after about eleven tomorrow morning. Those keys should arrive first thing tomorrow morning, and once they arrive you can start that awful drive. Don't forget Dominic, the lazy ass, hasn't fixed the lock as of yet. It might stick a little, so don't be afraid to jiggle the key. He swears to have it fixed by the time we leave, but I'm not holding my breath. Oh, and one more thing—"

"Mmmm?"

"Be careful in the woods Thursday night. It's the full moon."

"Oh. Right. Sure."

Chloe wasn't really sure what more to say. She believed Mary, who insisted Dominic was a werewolf. Yet at the same time, she didn't believe her. It was rather confusing and she didn't think about it much. Mary had assured her they weren't the werewolves of movies—insane killers and feasters of flesh. But rather, insisted they were mostly normal men, who happened to turn into wolves and run around in the huge national park on the evenings of the full moon.

Chloe didn't like to think of it any more than she wanted to think about Dominic's brother, Samuel. She had been Mary's bridesmaid, and Samuel had been the groomsman. She had spent most of the wedding avoiding the drop-dead handsome man.

It had been the strangest feeling, walking down the aisle ahead of Mary, feeling proud and sad at the same time. She was overjoyed for Mary finally finding the love she deserved. Yet, having her brother and cousin moving to the other side of the state to be with this family had made her feel slightly odd.

She was happy for them, but sad at the same time. She wasn't sure what she thought of the large, boisterous family. She certainly liked them, but also resented them slightly. That resentment ate at her and made her feel awful and mean.

She had been determined to like and get to know the family her cousin was marrying into, and had been doing an admirable job—until she had met the elusive Samuel. Standing next to Dominic, in a navy blue suit just like his brothers, he had taken her breath away.

Taller by a few inches than Dominic, he was lean and athletically muscled. His shoulder-length hair had been restrained into a short ponytail. Staring at him, he made her heart stutter out an unusual rhythm, and, temporarily, she wondered if she would faint from lack of oxygen.

Quickly snapping back to reality, she continued to her designated spot a little faster than the priest had asked. Watching Mary walk down the aisle, her face alight, looking beautiful in her wedding gown, Chloe forgot Samuel and concentrated on her cousin.

The rest of the afternoon, however, hadn't been so easy. Samuel hadn't been an easy man to ignore, sadly for her peace of mind. They had politely conversed through a number of light, noncommittal subjects such as the weather, and didn't Mary look stunning, throughout the small reception.

Yet the underlying sexual tension between them had been almost impossible to ignore. She was sure he felt it too—yet when he made no mention of it, she stubbornly refused to bring it up either.

Chloe had quickly left the following morning after helping Mary pack for her brief honeymoon. She had been trying desperately not to think of Samuel ever since.

Somewhere inside her, she was honest enough to acknowledge that part of the reason she accepted Mary's invitation to spend the extended weekend in the cabin was the potential to meet up with Samuel again—maybe to try and sort out the strange chemistry between them.

Chloe had no intention of fucking him out of her system—look where that had got Mary! Married to the man.

Yet for six interminable months as she taught twelve and thirteen year old children to bake cookies and muffins, and safely use an oven and burners, the wretched man had hovered around the edges of her thoughts, teasing her at odd moments and causing more than a few nights of intensely erotic dreams and consequential early morning cold showers.

More and more she had found herself thinking of him last thing at night and would wake up with him on her mind early in the morning.

It was slowly driving her insane and ruining her for other men. She had finally had enough. She didn't have a particular plan, but her plans rarely panned out anyway. She would simply wing it, like so much of her life.

"Helloooo, you still there? Have you even heard a word I've said?"

Chloe cleared her throat.

"Umm...sorry. I was zoning."

Mary sighed.

"Just remember to be careful driving over, okay? Go grab a pen and paper, brat, I'll give you detailed, explicit instructions so even you couldn't get lost."

Laughing, Chloe stretched for the pen and pad of paper she always kept near the phone. If nothing else, four days in the secluded cabin would be perfect for her to catch up on her reading. Her pile of books to-be-read had dramatically increased over the last six months, threatening to take over her small room.

Jotting down directions and odds and ends she thought of to pack, Chloe smiled at her cousin's thoughtfulness. Even if she didn't manage to talk to Samuel, an extended weekend of rest and contemplation was exactly what she needed to recharge her batteries.

Chapter One
Late Thursday Evening

ഗ

Chloe had been driving for what felt like years—or weeks at the very least. Her eyes were gritty, her arms and legs ached from being cramped in her small car for hours and hours with only toilet breaks. She desperately wished for a decently cooked meal, and not drive-thru rubbish.

Ten minutes ago she had just turned onto the gravel road her directions stated ran past the outskirts of the park. From what Mary said, ten miles up this main road was the turnoff to Artemais and William's house. About a mile before that was a much smaller dirt track leading to a narrow, winding road that split. Left was to Dominic's cabin, right was to his brother, Samuel's cabin.

The throbbing ache behind Chloe's eyes grew worse as she strained to catch a glimpse of a sign. Sighing, she pulled her small car over off the road. With one thing after another, it had taken her forever to get on the road. It would be beyond stupid if she crashed her car into a tree less than ten miles from her destination.

It was already past midnight, another twenty minutes to stretch her legs and relieve herself wasn't going to make much difference. Besides, her needs had passed beyond urgent about an hour back.

The full moon hung so low and bright in the sky she decided not to take her flashlight with her. Pulling her huge coat from the backseat, she locked the car and looked left and right. The woods were far more dense on the left. Knowing she would only be going fifty feet or so into them, she wrapped herself up in her coat and headed towards them, eager for *any* sort of break to stop the monotony of simply driving along the road.

When her small car was only just barely out of sight, she stopped and looked around the moonlit woods. It truly was beautiful. The moonlight and stars above glowed down onto the earth, as if bathing it in its safety and care. The forest felt alive. Small animals made noises, owls hooted, and Chloe could almost feel the tension and life hidden beneath the surface.

Smiling, she stretched her legs and rubbed her eyes, taking a few more steps into the woods, being careful not to stray too far.

Maybe ten, maybe fifteen minutes later as many of the kinks as she could fix had left her legs. At least her more immediate problem of her filled bladder was also taken care of.

Her back still ached from all the driving, but at least her eyes had adjusted to the beauty of the woods and felt slightly less gritty. Reluctantly, she admitted to herself she would a) freeze to death and b) be eaten alive by bugs if she simply lay down in this beautiful woodland area and fell asleep.

Deciding to try and remember the placement of this beautiful spot to revisit later, Chloe began to turn back to her car when she caught the white glow of another human. Startled, Chloe stopped. Thinking it must be another person, maybe lost in the woods, she was about to call out and offer help, when the man turned around and she recognized who it was.

Samuel.

He was so handsome it was hard to catch her breath for a moment. His chest was bare, giving off a pale glow from the reflected moonlight. Even though he had a light tan, in the silvery moonlight he looked ghostlike, pale. Her mouth dried up, and Chloe couldn't move her eyes, even when he began to unbuckle and remove his jeans.

Her lust-numbed mind briefly wondered why the hell he was standing in the middle of the forest, stark naked, but she was enjoying the view far, far too much to be too bothered by it.

Chloe rested against a convenient tree, licked her lips and prayed he would stand like that for another twenty minutes or so while she looked her fill. He really was a most stunning man. Why the hell hadn't some lucky woman snapped him up yet?

He obviously hadn't seen her yet, and she liked that just fine. Being able to watch him without him knowing of her presence made her feel decadent, naughty. His shoulder-length dark brown hair glowed darkly in the moonlight, caressing his shoulders in a flirty way she briefly envied.

Why was it men's hair always behaved, no matter how badly they treated it, yet women would pamper and coddle their hair from age about ten onwards, yet it *never* did what they required from it? Men with long hair never had bad hair days. Or bed hair. Chloe smiled as she mentally recited the indignities women put up with.

The thought of bed hair briefly sidetracked her, however, and made her wonder how Samuel would look, rumpled, first thing in the morning after a long, intense night of loving. The mental pictures whizzing through her mind had her blood heating and the chill of the night air suddenly became a much-needed breeze rather than a freezing wind.

Far too soon for Chloe's liking, Samuel started stretching his muscles and shimmering.

Shimmering?

Chloe rubbed her eyes, damning how tired and worn out she felt after a full day of driving. If the gorgeous hunk in front of her was shimmering she must be far more tired than she realized. Maybe she should just bunk down for the night in her small car.

One minute Chloe was rubbing her eyes, hoping to refocus on all that gorgeous naked masculinity, the next she was staring open-mouthed at the largest wolf she had *ever* seen.

The wolf was huge, far larger than the few specimens she had watched at a safe distance behind a fence at a zoo or parkland reserve. Chloe frantically looked around for where the naked Samuel could have disappeared to.

He was nowhere to be seen.

That so did not happen. I'm overtired. Or over-stressed. Or something. No way in Hell did Samuel just turn into a wolf before my very eyes.

Too panicked to think about anything except the instant denial hammering in her brain, Chloe stood rooted to the spot.

When the wolf-Samuel—*he is* so *not that wolf*, her brain injected—turned to stare directly at her, then sniff the air, Chloe couldn't help the girlish gasp that escaped her lips.

Oh shit, he's scenting me.

Unsure and uncaring where the thought came from, Chloe tried to gather her wits.

The wolf silently padded over to her. Frozen in terror, Chloe mentally begged her legs to run, to move. Never in all her years had she felt so terrified she could not move. She had always been in full control of her body. She didn't enjoy the feeling of helplessness her terror caused her.

In less than a minute, the wolf had come right up to her. Yet it was not growling, its hairs were not raised in anger or threat. Chloe blinked, totally confused.

Why wasn't the animal threatening her?

Like a gigantic dog, the wolf stuck its muzzle into her hand, making her pet his head. Despite herself, Chloe felt the warm, silky fur covering the giant beast. For the barest moment, wolf and woman stood in the woods, frozen together.

When a piercing howl broke the silence of the night, Chloe snapped back to reality.

She was standing in the middle of the woods petting a wolf.

Bad idea girl, the big bad wolf ATE Red Riding Hood's grandmother.

Jerking her hand back from the silky head of the wolf, she turned and fled back to her car.

For a few paces the wolf loped after her, as if they were playing a game of Chase. As her car came into view, she continued running, panting for breath and the wolf fell behind. Digging her keys from the pocket of her coat, Chloe rushed to open her door. Jerking it open, she was about to jump in, when some niggling sensation made her pause and turn back.

The wolf stood there, on the edge of the forest line. Fierce and proud, he stood watching her. Woman and beast stared at each other for a moment, while time seemed to stand still.

Chloe was scared, but unafraid at the same time. It was the strangest sensation. Not once had the beast growled at her, threatened her in any way, yet he was a wild beast, who hunted and killed smaller animals. And when that wolf in the distance had howled, she had felt very much lower on the food chain.

Coming to her senses, she climbed into her small car, closed the door and roared the engine. Dirt spewing everywhere, she made a 180 degree turn, coming perilously close to a number of trees, and headed back out of the forest.

Driving as fast as she dared, she headed back down to the main freeway, as far away as possible from the strange sensations that Samuel and that wolf had invoked in the forest.

Chapter Two

Samuel stared at the retreating car. Strangely, he felt relieved and sad at the same time. Since first catching sight of Chloe Dennison at her cousin and his brother's wedding, she had been invading his thoughts and his mind.

This unnerved him on a number of levels. His gut screamed in warning that she was his One, his mate. No matter how hard he tried to push that thought away, it crept back to haunt him at the most unusual times, mostly just before he closed his eyes to sleep at night.

It also unnerved him from the knowledge that she alone could change his well-structured world. Samuel freely admitted he loved his life. He had his freedom in his own small cabin, yet with the vibrancy and love of his family so close at hand when needed. Largely he lived as he pleased, and while he worked hard and well, he still retained plenty of time to party just as hard and still do the things that pleased him.

If his three brothers were any indication, when one mated and fell in love, one became a blindsided sap. Samuel loved his brothers, and liked and respected their respective mates. Yet surrounded by so much mush and happiness, he couldn't help but wonder if they had all lost their minds.

Any woman who could mess with his well-ordered and much loved world posed a problem. Yet even knowing this, Samuel still found himself entranced with Chloe, wondering what it would be like to have her wild in his arms, to scream for him and arch into his body…

Musing so long on his human thoughts, the wolf instincts of Samuel's current form finally kicked in.

He raised his head to the full moon, drawn in by her glow and beauty. The scents of the forest seemed to suddenly come back to life, and his mind was easily, thankfully diverted.

Contemplation could come later. Right now he simply *had* to follow the rabbit as it darted across his peripheral vision and chase it down.

Bounding off, Samuel felt relieved to let his wolf side take over his human one. Mooning over Chloe Dennison was not how he wanted to spend his evening.

* * * * *

Chloe pulled up to Dominic and Mary's small cabin. After drinking the last of the herbal tea in her thermos and eating her last granola bar, she had come to her senses.

She had been a moron.

Sure, it had taken her the best part of forty minutes hell-for-leather driving, twenty minutes of munching and drinking almost-cold tea, and another hour driving back, but at three a.m., who the hell was counting?

Deep inside herself, she had known since her conversation with Mary that the Rutledge men were…different. Seeing it up close and personal wasn't a cakewalk, but neither was she a swooning southern belle from some cheesy, cheap novel. She was a mature twenty-six, had held any number of jobs, and was a capable, efficient modern woman.

What was a little fur between friends? It wasn't as if she would be seeing much of any of the Rutledge brothers. She was here for some quiet contemplation. She needed to make some goals, sketch out some plans.

Like most other women, she had always assumed she would graduate from school, get a job, meet some nice young man, get married, and have kids and work part-time to put them through a decent college.

Instead, she had worked through a large number of jobs, unable to settle down in one area. Mary insisted it was because she hadn't found her passion, hadn't found her niche. Chloe, in return, insisted it was because she simply didn't have a long attention span and got bored easily. What was the use of settling down in one job when so many had such appeal?

Chloe knew she needed to reassess her goals, make some plans for the next five years. She needed to find where her passion lay, and find something she could happily settle on doing for the next few years.

In any event, she couldn't turn around and drive the long distance home, certainly not because she got a little scared seeing Samuel turning into a wolf. Mary would never have sent her here if the men were dangerous when they turned.

A few howls and a bit of a shock was a small price to pay in return for a long weekend in seclusion, with nothing more stressful than reading and self-reflection on the menu.

Chloe picked up her small backpack, with her necessities and a few half-read books, and opened the car door. A long, hot shower and a long night of sleep would restore her brain capacity. The following morning was soon enough to unpack the trunk and get her larger bag, also filled with books and a few changes of clothes. Mary had insisted on filling her fridge and cupboards with food, so she hadn't bothered to bring more than her favorite chocolate bars with her.

Crunching her way up to the front door of the cabin, she pulled out the spare keys Mary had lent her. Fiddling around in the moonlight, she found the correct key for the front door.

Inserting it in the door, she was briefly surprised when it didn't turn the lock. Remembering Mary's warning of how the lock sometimes stuck, she jiggled the key around, leaning on it to give it more pressure.

When neither maneuver budged the key even an inch, she swore under her breath. Chloe stepped back under the bright light of the full moon and checked the other two keys.

Neither of them would open the door, so the first key must be correct.

Trying once more, jiggling the key with as much force as she dared, she eventually pulled back in disgust. Staring at the lock, Chloe realized it had a dead bolt, effectively squashing her chances of being able to pick the lock open.

Sighing heavily, Chloe pocketed the useless keys and walked around the side of the dark cabin to find an accessible window. It was cold, she was tired, and she refused to sleep the night away in her small car, even if she had thought about it earlier.

All she wanted was a long, hot shower and a soft, warm bed. Chloe knew she was fairly proficient at picking locks, but surely some of the windows would be accessible?

Finding the perfect window, Chloe peered in the room. The pale moonlight made shadows, but she thought this was the bedroom. Pulling her lock picks out of her backpack, grateful she always kept them handy for practice; she easily opened the small catch and raised the window.

Muttering curses about Mary under her breath, Chloe threw her small backpack onto the floor wincing at the *thud* of it falling to the floor. Taking a deep breath to steady herself, she rested her hands on the windowsill.

Thankful she had worn only her old black jeans and a light sweater for the long drive, she easily pulled her lithe frame up through the window. Panting with the exertion, dragging a bit of dust with her, she landed with a thud on the cabin floor next to her bag. Standing quickly and brushing the barely existent dust from her jeans, Chloe turned around to close and lock the window behind her, a tired but happy grin on her face.

Just as she lowered the window, she felt thick, heavy arms trap her own arms at her side and lift her from the ground. Before she could even think of her self-defense moves,

Chloe found herself being held firmly on a soft bed, a large, heavy body pressing her into the mattress.

Desperately trying to push up against the wide shoulders, Chloe found the mattress made poor leverage.

"Since when did you take up breaking and entering, little girl?"

Chloe felt the tension seep out of her body. *Samuel.*

"Since the keys Mary gave me didn't fit her damned front door. Since when did you need to use brute force to get a little action?" Chloe felt her breath hitch as laughter rumbled through Samuel's chest, still firmly pressed up against her breasts.

"I don't need force, little girl. I merely didn't want you trying those silly self-defense moves on me, potentially giving me a bruise. Mary has been very vocal in her pride on your self-defense skills."

Chloe squirmed. If she could just get some sort of leverage...but with her entire lower body twined in Samuel's and her arms caged in his huge embrace, she didn't hold out much hope.

"What are you doing here?" he breathed in her ear. The teasing puff of his breath made her heart beat accelerate wildly. Chloe couldn't tell if she was annoyed or incredibly turned on by the situation.

If the heated blood flowing through her system and the dampness in her panties were any indication, she had a sinking sensation she was more turned on than offended by the heavy press of Samuel's body.

Unfortunately, much as she would love to shed her clothes and inhibitions, she didn't think simply having a fling with this man would work, certainly not in the long term. Mary had insisted on merely having one night with Dominic. Nearly a year later they were happily married and expecting their first child.

So much for a one-night stand with a Rutledge man!

Chloe took a deep breath, the one from the bottom of her diaphragm her Tai Chi instructor had taught her a number of years ago. A calming breath.

"I needed a break. Mary offered me the use of her cabin, as she and Dominic are going away for the long weekend. I didn't realize you'd be sitting inside it waiting for me. May I get up now?"

She couldn't see Samuel's expression in the dark, but she could almost feel his puzzlement, the weight of his stare as he looked at her. She dug into her jeans pocket, withdrawing the keys Mary had lent her that had been so useless.

"Here. Mary's keys. Believe me now?"

Suddenly, Samuel's large, comforting weight was removed from her body and she simply lay on the bed.

"My apologies. But obviously you got the directions incorrect. This is *my* cabin. Not Dom's. You must have made a wrong turn at the fork in the road."

Chloe felt heat rise in her cheeks. What he must think of her! Panting after him like every other bimbo he encountered. Well, she would squash *that* rumor before it could truly begin.

"I…umm…well! I must be off, lots of sleep to catch up on, and it is rather late. Sorry for intruding…"

Wriggling off the bed, she stepped quickly over to where her backpack still lay by the window, scooped it up and turned in what she hoped was the direction of the door.

Before she could take another step, Samuel's large, lean body blocked her way.

"Hmm…I haven't been real hospitable, have I? Shame on me. Dom *would* be upset; and Artemais would shake his head in that arrogant way of his. Let me make this up to you for my earlier lack of manners."

"Oh no, no! Really. If the situations had been reversed and a strange man had crawled through my window I'd have done the same thing. Honestly! I'll just head back down the road and crash at Mary's."

Samuel took a step closer to her, causing her to step backwards. Another step, and she was backed up against the wall.

"Uh, Samuel."

Very carefully, he leaned both hands against the wall, effectively caging her for the second time this evening.

She could feel the heat in his body—feel it radiating to ensnare her, draw her closer to him. Despite herself, she closed her eyes and breathed the scent of him into her, enjoying the masculine warmth he emitted.

She felt her legs tremble. The desire to give in to temptation and wrap her arms around him, to pull him closer, was immense.

"Samuel, this really won't work. I didn't come out here to start some sort of sexual odyssey with you."

Chloe cringed as he began to nibble his way down her neck, right into that sensitive spot at the juncture of neck and shoulder. Hearing the breathiness in her voice, she cleared her throat and tried again.

"Seriously. I'm here to look at my options. I need some personal time, personal space. I...uh...need to...*ooh*...make plans..."

Chloe gave up trying to speak as Samuel ran his hands up and down her sides, fitting them into the groove of her curves. Just the lightest touch of his hands—even through her jeans and thin sweater—sent electric thrills racing through her.

It was the most bizarre feeling, but she could swear she felt the electric attraction rush between them. It was as if they were connected somehow through their lust and mutual attraction.

"I've been thinking of this since the wedding. You were always so careful to not get caught with me alone. Did you really think you could avoid this? Avoid me, little girl?"

Chloe wanted to protest the endearment. Yet he didn't say "little girl" with contempt or patronizingly. It was said caressingly, as an acknowledgement of the almost ten year difference between their ages.

For a moment she considered pretending uneasiness at the large difference between their ages. From one gasp to the next she discarded the idea. She doubted she could carry off the outraged maiden act. He would undoubtedly know she was quite mature for her age and always preferred company of anyone, male or female, a number of years older than herself.

"I would hardly call twenty-six 'little', Samuel."

"At almost thirty-seven it seems young enough."

Chloe shivered. His voice was so sexy! Mary had mentioned he sang vocals for their band. She could well understand that voice crooning, beckoning, to females everywhere. Thankfully, it was that thought more than any other that snapped her back to reality.

The thought of the hundreds of other women who had fallen under his spell; the thought of that beautiful voice and sensually caressing hands being used on hordes of other women, was better than a bucket of cold water.

Chloe pulled herself back. Samuel still retained hold of her body, but his lips were thankfully not connected anymore.

"I need to be heading back to Dominic's cabin. I have to call Mary, leave her a message to say I've arrived safely."

"Call her from here."

Chloe rolled her eyes and dodged out of his embrace. Samuel was a heady temptation, she needed the fresh air to cool her off.

"Sure. Have *your* number come up on her cell phone's caller ID. I don't think so."

She could feel the weight of Samuel's stare on her back as she crossed the room to pick up her backpack. Seeing the messed up bed sheets as she passed back by the bed made her blush.

Even though he couldn't have been asleep for *that* long, as it had only been less than two hours since she had last seen him, she felt that strange sensation of having woken the sleeping wolf in his lair.

Maybe if she could simply get out of here and sort her screaming hormones out, she could start to relax again. Briefly, she wondered if she had packed her vibrator and spare batteries.

As she scooped up her bag, mentally running through what she had packed, and then unpacked, it took a moment for Samuel pulling on a sweater and sneakers to register.

"What are you doing?"

"Putting on sneakers and a sweater. It's a bit nippy outside."

"Don't be stupid, you're not coming with me."

Samuel raised an eyebrow cockily.

"Of course I am. Dominic would have my head if I simply let you run wild outside alone. A gentleman always escorts his lady home, or so Artemais and William have always insisted."

"But—"

"Besides, there's a shortcut I can show you. It's not precisely a track, but your car will get through it with no problems if I drive."

Chloe sighed. Arguing with him would only delay them longer. "And you can walk back by yourself?"

Samuel grinned cheekily. Instead of answering yes or no, he simply stated, "It's only a little over a mile."

Satisfied she could withstand any further seduction attempts, Chloe nodded and slung her backpack over her shoulder. She was tired and hated sleeping through the day. If she didn't get to bed really soon, the dawn would crack before she crawled into bed and sleep would become impossible.

"Then lead on, Macduff."

"Ooh, Shakespeare. Be careful, little girl, or you might just turn me on."

Chloe laughed and rolled her eyes, slamming the door shut behind them.

Chapter Three

ဆ

Chloe cringed at how easily Mary's keys turned the lock in her *real* front door. Dominic must have fixed the lock after all. Chloe sighed; she could be *such* a moron sometimes. She must be more tired than she realized.

Swinging the door open, she turned around, slightly breathless at the nearness of Samuel and his large body.

"Thanks for the escort. I think I can take it from here."

Switching on the hall light, she illuminated the foyer and main room. From the front door, she could see the kitchen and living room, and the small hall that led into the bedrooms.

Turning back with a firm smile planted on her face, she looked up to Samuel. He was studying her, his eyes roving over her face as if searching for something. She started mentally reciting French conjugation, determined not to let a speck of the lust she felt show in her eyes.

His deep blue eyes glowed with a heat and hunger. Chloe wondered if French conjugation was enough to keep the insane feelings of lust out of her eyes and mind.

Samuel leaned forward, and planted a soft kiss on her cheek. She felt heat swell up inside her again. *How the hell does he do this to me? One tiny caress and I simply melt inside?*

Chloe pressed her lips together, determined not to moan or give herself away in any other way. As he pulled back, she could see the male amusement in his eyes.

"I assume you'll want to go on some long walks tomorrow morning, to aid your *contemplation* and search, right?"

Frowning at the mental jumps needed to following his reasoning, Chloe simply nodded. "Probably, though not too early as it's rather close to dawn right now. Why?"

"I'll come by around breakfast time, lead you around. An unwary little girl could get lost in these big woods. We wouldn't want a big bad wolf to gobble you all up, now would we?"

Chloe stepped back, so she stood fully inside the cabin.

"The only big bad wolf around these parts is *you*, Mr. Rutledge. I'm not afraid of you, Samuel. Neither am I one of your stupid groupie girls, desperate to fall neatly into the palm of your hand. Sure. Come by tomorrow, or rather today, around nine. We can go on a nice long walk, and then you can leave me alone for the rest of the day. Deal?"

"The rest of the day?" he repeated. Nodding, he conceded to her wishes. "We have a deal. Until later, Chloe."

With that, he stepped back and Chloe shut the door, resisting the impulse to slam it in his face.

She'd show him! He obviously thought he could seduce her with barely a word or gesture. Well she had much bigger fish to fry this weekend. Handling one horny Rutledge man should be easy when faced with all the things she wanted to organize in her life.

Taking a lovely hot, though damnably brief shower, Chloe breathed deeply in her meditation and calming exercises. The shower more than anything else helped her relax, made it far easier for herself to slip into that sleepy, hazy state. Curling up in the soft guest bed, she left the curtains open, wanting to have the last of the moonlight glow protectively over her as she slept. She wasn't sure what was so soothing about the moonlight tonight of all nights, but it made her feel protected and loved.

She slept deeply and dreamlessly.

Chapter Four
Friday Midmorning

ℰᴑ

Samuel leaned over the kitchen counter and tried not to leer at Chloe. In snug-fitting jeans and a brightly patterned sweater, she made a cheerful picture first thing in the morning. She was running a brush through her light brown locks, the early morning sunlight highlighting blonde tresses among the brown.

Samuel found himself captivated by the simple action of her running the brush through her hair. He squashed a slightly disappointed feeling when she pulled back the mass into a ponytail, ending the little show.

"Ready to go walk, little girl?"

Chloe rolled her eyes, causing him to grin. He could tell from her drawn out groans and overreaction that she didn't *really* object to him calling her "little girl". She would have decked him, or tried to deck him he consoled himself, if she really had a serious problem with it.

The overreaction, the rolling of her gorgeous eyes, the loud, long sighs were all indications that while she might not enjoy the nickname, she didn't really want to admit to liking it. Even with the potential to upset her, the reaction he elicited from her every time he called her the endearment tempted him to continue.

It had been a long time since he'd sexually craved a woman whom he felt comfortable enough with to tease and taunt. It made the hunt that much more enjoyable.

This particular hunt seemed to be so unique, so tempting and exciting, he felt himself enjoying all sorts of things and thoughts he had never previously entertained.

His brain shied away from its knowledge of just how very different this particular hunt was becoming. Time enough to ponder *those* sort of thoughts later.

Samuel blinked. Chloe had walked over to the back door of the cabin and was standing there, waiting for him.

"Having second thoughts? Surely such a *little* girl as me can't be a threat to your masculine ego?"

Samuel grinned and dropped a hasty, chaste kiss on her cheek as he walked past her out the door.

"Not at all. I fully intend to have to carry you part of the way back here. I plan to take you on a circular trail Dom and I often run through when we feel particularly energetic."

Chloe laughed and slammed the back door behind her, throwing the lock without thinking about it.

"I can't wait to make you eat those words! You have no idea what sort of feminine monster you're creating here."

Samuel laughed and led them both down a narrow, barely there trail.

"It will certainly be interesting to see whose knees give out first—won't it?"

Enjoying his double entendre, and the blush that appeared on Chloe's cheeks, the pair set off into the woods.

* * * * *

"That was absolutely fantastic, thank you, Samuel."

Still unbelieving of the amount of energy she held inside that slight frame, Samuel took the keys to the cabin from her hand. Gallantly opening the door for her, he stepped aside to let her enter first.

"You're a lot more fit than I realized, little girl. How the hell can you do a six mile hike on an empty stomach, talk the *entire* time and still not be out of breath by the end?"

As Chloe brushed past him he felt his cock harden even more. Samuel had grown increasingly sexually frustrated as the walk had worn on. He had assumed his physical strength would be much greater than Chloe's. Through the long night, he had entertained any number of fantasies, all strangely revolving around Chloe getting tired and needing them both to stop for frequent rests.

He could have massaged her aching legs, or back, run his hands all over her smooth, lovely skin. Admittedly, most of his fantasies had led him to stripping her of her clothes and making passionate love to her on the grass of the forest floor, but a man needed goals!

Instead, Chloe had kept pace with him. While he had shortened his stride to make it easier for her, he still had been quite surprised at how easily she had kept up with him. He hadn't the heart to set too punishing a pace, yet neither had they dawdled.

Even harder for him had been following Chloe's conversation. She neatly sidestepped all his sexual innuendos, making him feel like a gauche thirteen-year-old again. She also diverted each and every personal topic of conversation he initiated.

Instead, she rambled on about her schoolchildren, the home economics class she had taught the previous semester, and the numerous other jobs she had held down over the last few years.

He had found himself disturbingly entranced with her humor and witty outlook on life. She freely laughed at herself and some of her clumsier antics, joked about her inability to sustain interest in a single job, and basically chattered on, blithely unaware of the reaction his body had to her nearness and scent.

Subtlety being his middle name, Samuel had tried to delve deeper into Chloe and her views, hoping to find a reason for his fierce attraction to her. He understood why he was physically aware of her, but he couldn't put his finger on the deeper attraction she held for him.

Irritatingly, the closest to personal conversation she had shared had been after his comment of how varied her jobs had been. She insisted Mary's opinion of her never having found where her passion lay was partially correct, but also the fact she had never taken a job diverse and interesting enough to hold her attention.

This rang true to his mind, as Chloe was a bubbly, full-of-life girl. It stood to reason that she would need a job that was dynamic, so she would be constantly challenged and surprised.

Yet, still he hungered for more knowledge of her—and not just in a sexual sense.

The more sexually aware of this amazing woman he became, the more frustrated he felt at her refusal to speak to him on more than a casual basis. It was as if she were holding him at arm's length.

As she possibly should.

Samuel had no idea of what he wanted from her. He didn't want to mate and settle down, yet the more time he spent in her presence, the more appeal that heretofore disgusting thought had.

Samuel gently shut the door behind him as he followed Chloe into Dom and Mary's small cabin. He honestly admitted to himself he was one confused puppy. He didn't want to settle down, yet he craved Chloe with a fierceness he wouldn't be able to suppress for long.

However, instead of chasing him and throwing herself at him like every other woman he had known, she was holding him at arm's length and insisting on the most casual and platonic of relationships.

None of his brothers had ever warned him women were such contrary creatures! He had quietly, and at the most annoyingly interesting times not-so-quietly, laughed at each of his brothers, in turn, when they had fallen hard and fast for their respective women.

He had fully supported them, while relishing the role of being able to jeer and tease each of them. The thought of turning to them now for help in sorting himself out was enough to make him turn an interesting shade of green.

"I suppose since I demolished all your weak-little-woman fantasies and made a positive step forward for your understanding of feminism at its best, the least I could do is cook you up some brunch, huh? It's a tad late to call it breakfast."

Samuel tried not to drool at the picture Chloe made in front of him. In a midriff T-shirt, jeans and hiking boots, she looked fresh and clean, despite the taxing hike they had just taken. A few stray wisps of hair escaped her ponytail, but otherwise she looked fresh from the shower.

"I never held weak-little-woman fantasies about you. On the contrary, I have little use for weak women. They tend to have insufficient stamina for a man of my tastes."

Chloe opened the fridge and began removing items, stacking them in partial disarray on the counter. She merely *harrumphed* her assent, refusing to rise to his sexual bait again.

Samuel felt surprised at the amount of food piling up on the counter. Bacon, eggs, hash browns, sausages, tomatoes…just like the sorcerer's apprentice the food kept on coming.

With her head stuck in the fridge, Samuel admired her ass. While Dominic was generally held to be the ass-man of the family, Samuel had to admit in this case he could see his brother's affinity for a luscious ass.

"You really didn't expect me to keep pace with you, did you?"

Samuel pulled his mind from the gutter and tried to concentrate on Chloe's conversation.

"You have to admit, it's not everyday one comes across a woman not only willing, but able to go on long hikes in the forest not long after the crack of dawn. It's not generally held to be a female accomplishment."

Slamming the fridge shut, Chloe rolled her eyes.

"Oh please. It mightn't be important to your little groupies, but some modern women enjoy being fit. Going to the gym is a great pastime many women enjoy nowadays. Trust me, if you go to the gym long enough, no matter how lazy you are, you soon become fit, whether you want to or not."

Samuel laughed. "Speaking from personal experience?"

"Absolutely. I am the Queen of sitting on the bicycle machines and either reading or watching the latest soap. Who needs all those silly weight-lifting machines anyway? Too much like hard work for me."

Samuel sat at the bench and watched as Chloe started cracking eggs and laying strips of bacon into the pan. She had unknowingly given him more information in that one scornful sentence than in the long hike they had just taken.

Yet watching her crack eggs into the pan and begin to lay out bacon strips seemed like such a homey scene, Samuel didn't know if the flutter in his stomach was arousal or panic.

What the hell was he doing? He certainly couldn't just seduce this woman and cast her aside. Not only would Mary cut off his balls, but Dominic would undoubtedly go a few rounds outside with him as well.

Even with this knowledge hammering the inside of his skull, the thought of *not* becoming intimate with Chloe had him breaking out in a sweat of panic. For the first time since losing his virginity at the tender age of thirteen, Samuel had no idea what he was going to do or how he was going to go about seducing a woman.

"Helloooo, anyone home? Samuel, are you feeling okay? You're looking a little pale."

"I'm fine, just…uh…thinking about a…um…case I'm working on."

"Case? What are you working on now?"

Samuel perked up, back on well-known territory. Managing to look both offended and outraged at the same time, he clasped a hand over his heart.

"No! Please don't tell me you have been a part of this family for nearly six months now and no one has told you my life story."

Chloe returned her attention to the eggs and laughed.

"Matthew only talks about Dominic and how marvelous his computer skills are and how dull college is compared to working with you both. I know you're a private eye of some sort, so go on and boast away, tell me about this so-interesting case of yours."

Samuel shrugged and sat back into his seat. Watching Chloe set up the eggs, bacon, sausages and hash browns onto two large plates, he leaned over the counter to take out napkins and cutlery for them both.

"Much of the work we do is fairly regular. Taking photos, following people to gather evidence for custody battles, or to help one party of a divorce get alimony from the other party. Exposing fraudulent worker's compensation claims, etcetera, etcetera. Dominic, and to a smaller extent Matthew, take care of the more computer side of the business. Searching out hackers, updating and protecting the security company and clients."

Chloe sat down and indicated for him to dig in. Spearing a mouthful of eggs, Samuel closed his eyes and moaned as they melted on his tongue. He tried to think the last time someone other than his sisters-in-law had cooked for him.

He might be having trouble working out exactly what he wanted with Chloe, but in that instant he knew he would be doing his damnedest to keep her around for a while. Women who cooked, and cooked well in particular, were thin on the ground nowadays.

A man needed priorities, and Chloe's cooking had instantly leapt right up to the top of his list, directly competing with making her come until she screamed, and having them both fuck madly until they expired from exhaustion.

Chapter Five

❧

Chloe watched Samuel put away a staggering amount of groceries. The man might be lean, but he ate enough food to keep an entire football team satisfied! A niggling voice at the back of her head insisted it was a dumb idea to feed him, that like a stray or wild animal, he'd keep on coming back for more now that she had relented and fed him once.

Surprisingly, even though she had no intention of letting him seduce her, the thought of Samuel coming back to keep her company didn't panic her. It's not as if he would force her, or rape her, and as long as she held some semblance of control, she was willing to play the game.

When the object of her thoughts finally sat back, let his cutlery drop onto his plate, and rested his hands smugly over his nonexistent belly, she smiled, satisfied.

"Sure you've had enough?"

Looking around the kitchen warily, Samuel raised an eyebrow.

"I thought that was all you cooked?"

"I think there are a few blueberry muffins in the pantry, if you're still hungry."

Startlingly, Samuel seemed to consider the notion for a moment. She raised her eyebrows, disbelieving.

"You can't *possibly* still be hungry?"

"Hey," he started, feigning offense, "I'm a man of healthy appetites."

Standing up, she picked up both their plates and cutlery. Rinsing them in the sink and placing them in the dishwasher,

Chloe took her time turning around. Crossing her arms over her chest, she leaned back against the sink.

"Well?"

"I might give the muffins a pass. You might want them for a snack later on."

Despite herself, Chloe grinned.

"You're too kind." She checked her watch. Nearly noon. Time to start some serious relaxing and reading.

Thankfully, Samuel seemed to take the hint. Standing, he stretched his tall, lean frame, scratching his belly in the self-satisfied way males around the world do after a decent home-cooked meal.

"Well, I'd best get off to work. It has been a true pleasure, and vastly interesting. I'll be back after sunset for a light supper. Want me to bring the wine?"

Caught off guard, Chloe took a moment for the words to sink in. "Excuse me?"

"Our deal, you said breakfasts and not during the days. That leaves the nights."

Shocked by his audacity, Chloe didn't know whether to laugh or throw a pan at the man.

"When I said you'd leave me alone the rest of the day, I meant you wouldn't be back at all. Breakfast was only supposed to be today, after the hike."

Samuel grinned down at her.

"Come on, love. You're going to go on a hike tomorrow morning too, surely?"

Chloe frowned. "Maybe, but I certainly wasn't planning on going with you. I don't think I could get too lost around here."

"Think of how much fun it will be. And as a reward for letting me tour you around the woods and small trails around here, you can help me try out this new game Dominic has found."

"What new game?"

"I'll bring it tonight. It's a kind of card game."

"I thought you had graduated from the high school mentality years ago. Surely don't expect me to fall for the old strip poker thing?"

Samuel laughed. "I don't think so, but there's no telling with Dominic. Come on, give it a shot. If you get offended or it really upsets you, I promise I'll leave when you order me away."

Chloe tilted her head, considering. She wasn't used to being totally alone. She enjoyed her freedom and having time to herself, but after a whole day of lazing around reading and thinking and going on much shorter hikes, she might enjoy the company.

It wasn't as if Samuel was going to seduce her, she wouldn't let him.

Anyway, it might be interesting to tease the beast and then send him away with a raging hard-on. "You swear you'll leave when I tell you to? No cajoling like this, no sad puppy dog eyes and pleas."

Samuel laughed. "I don't beg. Ever."

Chloe nodded. "Me either. You have a deal then. Come on over and we'll try out this game of Dominic's. I take it it's an 'adult game'?"

Samuel took Chloe's outstretched hand and shook on it.

"They're the only kind Dominic knows to my knowledge."

"Well, at least this shouldn't prove boring."

Walking Samuel over to the door, she let him kiss her cheek again in farewell. She stood and watched him walk back into the brush. The sunlight shone down brightly, but not too hot. When he was out of view, Chloe stalled a minute longer. Shaking her head and muttering to herself, she reentered the cabin, keeping the door open for the warm breeze.

Curling up on the couch she opened her first book. Determined, she skimmed the previous page and caught up on the hero and heroine's current predicament.

Ensnared, she began to read.

Chapter Six

ℰᴑ

Chloe opened the door that evening in the same jeans and bright sweater she had been in when he had left earlier that day. Samuel smiled, a bottle of red in one arm, a small box in his other hand.

"You don't waste any time, do you?"

Samuel looked behind him, and the just-set sun. The sky still held traces of pink, red, and orange from the spectacular sunset.

"Sun's set, hasn't it?"

Grinning, he held the bottle of red out to her.

"You eaten yet?"

Rolling her eyes, Chloe grabbed the bottle from him and stepped back to let him enter the cabin.

"Let me guess, you're one of those men who constantly eat? I did warn you I wouldn't cook anything other than breakfast. You should have eaten before you came over."

Chloe turned her cheek for Samuel's kiss as he entered the cabin. She frowned when she realized she now expected the chaste greeting. Slowly, she closed the door and turned to face Samuel.

She had better be careful, she warned herself, next thing she'd know she would start taking other liberties for granted. Samuel seemed to be growing on her when she wasn't paying attention.

Shaking herself, she remembered she was the person in charge here, not Samuel. He had promised not to step over the line she drew, and she trusted him to honor that promise.

As she raised her eyes to meet his, she saw him pleading silently. She doubted the man could read her mind—so he obviously was begging for food, not sex. Then again, knowing Samuel as she did, she bet he wouldn't turn down either if she offered.

She sighed. "I suppose I might have some cheese to go with this red. Let me check." Feeding the man currently seemed like the lesser of two evils.

Instantly the pleading look vanished, and Samuel shone a bright smile on her. "I knew you wouldn't let me starve. I brought the game. Here, I'll grab the glasses, you get the cheese and a cutter."

Chloe sighed, trying to hide her laughter, and headed into the kitchen. Digging into the fridge she found some cheese, way in the back. Silently heaping grateful blessing on Mary for the find, she found a sharp knife and a cutting board. As she headed back into the living room, Samuel had set the box on the coffee table and found two wineglasses.

Chloe eyed them, worried. "Weren't those wedding gifts? Can't we use something else? I'm much too likely to break them and that would really upset me."

"Nah. These are old drinking glasses of Dom's. It's what he used to use to impress the ladies he brought back here. I left the really good stuff back in the cabinet. Mary would likely try to skin me if we broke one of her precious crystal goblets."

Chloe nodded and sat down. Taking the smallish box from the table she opened it and looked through the cards as Samuel poured them both a glass of wine.

The cards seemed to be color-coded into three sections. Cards with a blue border each had the title *Beginner: Getting to know each other*, green borders held the title: *Medium: for a little more intimacy*, and red borders read *Advanced: for those who dare*.

Flicking through them, not reading them in any depth, Chloe understood enough to gather that some of the cards held dares and others simply had questions written on them. Putting the box of cards back, she looked at the cover.

A dating, getting-to-know-you game for all levels, the cover declared.

"So remind me again, why are we playing this game of Dominic's?"

Samuel handed her the glass of wine and sat back in his own chair. Clearing his throat, he looked almost sheepish for a moment. "Uh, it's not precisely Dominic's."

Chloe just sat back and waited for the rest of the explanation.

"You see, it *was* Dominic's game, but he sort of gifted me with it after he married Mary."

Chloe felt her stomach twist. "You mean he played this game with Mary? If this is something they did I'm not sure I really want to follow after them. The mental images won't be pretty."

Samuel started to blush, both worrying and amazing Chloe. "Uh…no…you don't fully understand. Dominic…used…this game before he met your cousin."

Blinking, Chloe finally fitted the pieces together. "Oh. I understand. It's one of those pick-up games? Where forced intimacy and a sharing of confidences brings a couple together. Eventually one thing leads to another and the couple end up in bed screwing madly. How close am I?"

Samuel cleared his throat. "Uh, fairly close, I believe."

Chloe nodded. "I'll remind you of your promise to leave when I've had enough."

Samuel nodded curtly.

Chloe shrugged. If Samuel was still willing to leave when she told him to, she didn't mind prying into his psyche. She was prepared to let him into a little of her mind as well. Fair was fair after all.

Choosing a blue card, Chloe sat back to read it thoroughly. Absently, she checked with Samuel.

"We're starting out on the blue ones, right? No sense in spoiling the fun and jumping the gun to the medium or advanced dares right away."

A strangled grunt was the only reply she got. Looking up, she saw Samuel's face scrunch as he sipped too much wine.

Shrugging, she returned to the card. *"What is your favorite sexual position?"*

Chloe turned the card over. The back was blue, the front white with the simple words written neatly. No indication was given as to whether Chloe answered the question herself or asked Samuel for his answer. Smiling, she figured with the lack of directions, she might as well make it up on the spot.

"So, Samuel," she purred, enjoying playing the vixen for once, "tell me *all* about your favorite sexual position."

Samuel took one more sip of his wine, then set the glass down on the coffee table. Sitting back, he removed his sneakers and relaxed his posture in the chair. Steepling his fingers to support his head, Samuel seemed to take the question very seriously.

"My *favorite*…hmmm…you certainly don't pull any punches, love. I suppose if I simply had to cut it down to one favorite position, I'd prefer the woman on top. I love seeing a lady astride me, pumping away, taking her pleasure and giving me incredible pleasure in return."

Chloe felt her mouth dry slightly at the mental images she found searing across her mind. Herself, astride Samuel, thrusting down upon him to make him reach deep, deep inside her. Licking her lips, she tried to drag her mind away from the heated images.

"Mmm…yeah…gotta admit a woman on top is probably my favorite position. What about you?"

"Pardon?"

"You, little girl. What's *your* favorite sexual position?"

162

Determined to be just as blatant and casual, Chloe sat back in her own chair, tucking her legs up underneath her. Mentally she ran through the list. Missionary was too ordinary, and though she enjoyed it, she liked to be a bit wild. Doggy style was fun, but certainly not her favorite. She enjoyed being on top, but refused to copy Samuel and appear as if she were copping out.

"I'm not sure it's my *favorite* favorite, but it certainly gets me hot and going every time. So I suppose in that sense it's the best. There's something about being backed into a wall that drives me crazy."

She paused for a second, gauging the reaction this caused in Samuel. A fire sparked in his deep blue eyes, hot and molten. She noticed his breaths were coming slightly faster, and every inch of his attention was firmly focused on her. Taking confidence in his obvious attention, she continued.

"One of the first sexual encounters I had was in a shower. We were rather inexperienced still, so it was more a farce than a heated sexual odyssey. But being gently backed up against the wall, with the water streaming down around us, even though we fumbled and groped, and the tiles were uncomfortably cold…it still gets me hot every time I think about it. I suppose it's got something to do with the fact that up against the wall has the naughty factor of a quickie, along with that 'woman under submission' thing without actually getting involved in all the bondage games."

She shrugged, blushing slightly. Samuel was still staring intently at her, soaking up every word and nuance. It made her feel a bit odd, being under his undivided attention. Determined to turn the spotlight from herself, and feeling as if she had certainly answered her part of the question fully, she waved her hand at him.

"Well, go on. Pick a card."

Samuel opened his mouth, but she glared at him and crossed her arms over her chest. She hadn't exactly meant to give quite so much detail to him. But now that she had, she refused to enter into more conversation about it. With luck, the next card would be a little less personal.

Who was she kidding? The voice inside her head silently mocked. *The game is designed to create intimacy,* she reminded herself. *Remember your own mocking of enforced intimacy bringing up situations like this?*

Chloe ignored her own doubts, and smiled brightly at Samuel, causing his eyes to narrow slightly. For a moment, she could swear he could hear the almost panicked fighting going on in her brain.

With a very small smile on his face, he leaned forward and picked up a blue- rimmed card at random. For a moment, he simply stared at it. Chloe stared at the black backing, wishing desperately that she too could read the card. She wasn't the most patient person on earth, and the excited suspense was driving her insane as the seconds ticked by.

After what was probably only a minute or so, but felt like a small eternity, Samuel huskily said, "What's you favorite time of day to do *it*?"

Chloe took a breath, unaware until then she had been holding it. *Her* favorite time? Did women have favorite times?

Thinking about it, Chloe realized she didn't really have one at all. For the right man under the right circumstances any time was her favorite time. She didn't, however, want to come across as a sex-craving maniac.

"Uh…well…assuming we're talking about someone I'm sexually interested in, first thing in the morning is always nice. It sort of starts the day off right, you know?" At Samuel's raised eyebrow, she continued. "And last thing at night is always nice. Relaxes you into a nice sleep with interesting dreams. Nothing wrong with having some nookie to complete a girl's day."

"Let me guess. You're also not opposed to a nooner now and then, or maybe middle of the afternoon perhaps?"

Chloe tried hard not to blush. "And how about you, Mr. Stud Muffin? Or maybe we should say when *isn't* your favorite time?"

Samuel's grin was slightly feral in its intensity. "Damn straight. With the right woman, *any* time is my favorite. There's nothing in that to be ashamed of. That's how you really feel, isn't it, little girl?"

Chloe nodded curtly, not knowing why it felt weird to admit it. She kept her eyes away from Samuel and reached forward to pick up her glass of wine.

"I guess so. I suppose I'd never really thought about it. With the right person it doesn't seem to matter what time it is when you get together, the sex is always good and always welcome. I think women are just expected to not want it all the time. Men can be a bit weird about that."

"Weird how?" Samuel also picked up his glass of wine, content to continue the conversation.

Chloe thought for a moment before she spoke. "Well, if a man is horny all the time, that's just expected. Men think about sex all the time, men want sex all the time. It's a fact of life and no one thinks they're strange if they admit to such. But for a woman, we're supposed to be...I don't know...more restrained, purer than that somehow. We're not supposed to daydream about sex all the time, or feel horny all the time. Women who do, throughout the ages, have been thought of as whores or sluts."

Chloe took a sip of her wine, watching Samuel digest what she had said.

"To a degree, yes, I think you're right. But I also think you'd be surprised at how many men would love to be with a woman who enjoys her sexuality, who knows what she wants and isn't afraid to go after it. Sexually, there are few things that are a greater turn-on to a man than a woman who would whisper in his ear naughty things she wants to do, and then proceeds to do them to herself or him."

He shifted uncomfortably in his chair. Chloe looked at him and realized he had a raging hard-on from their conversation.

She smiled. "I can see that it's one of your fantasies, anyway."

He smiled at her. "Chloe, it's not the thought of just anyone whispering naughty suggestions that's giving me this boner—it's the thought of what sort of naughty things *you* would whisper in my ear."

Startled, Chloe took another sip of wine to give her hands something to do. Before she could stop herself, she imagined some of the things she might whisper in his ear. She had always wanted to wear a dress with no panties on underneath, go out to dinner and casually whisper the secret into her partner's ear. Watch the reaction she received.

Or maybe whisper her fantasy of being taken hard and fast as soon as she and her partner entered her small apartment after a night out somewhere. That thought immediately brought back her fantasy and enjoyment of quickies up against the wall.

Strange how things tended to click together after a drink or two of wine, she silently laughed at herself.

Forcing her mind away from her heated fantasies, she reminded herself that a few nights with this man could be a dangerous game to play.

Clearing her throat, trying desperately hard not to squirm in her seat to relieve the wet ache between her legs, Chloe tried forcing her mind back to the *game* they were playing. Sharply realizing her turn had come again, Chloe leaned forward to take yet another card from the box.

Chapter Seven

∽

Samuel casually crossed one large leg up over the other in a vain attempt to hide his incredibly hard cock.

Chloe might be young when compared to his years, but her package sure packed a wallop. She was the perfect height for him, five-eight to his six-four, slim but curvy in all the required places. Not for the first time today, he wondered if it was genius or self-inflicted torture playing this game of cat and mouse with her.

He had never found himself particularly confused when contemplating the opposite sex. Either he wanted to bed them, and proceeded to do so to both party's mutual satisfaction, or he felt more a friendship bond rather than a sexual one, as he did with his few female friends and his sisters-in-law.

His uneasiness with Chloe, he was almost certain now, stemmed from the fact she didn't fit neatly in either box in his mind. He felt a sexual attraction to her, got a raging boner when he thought too much of her or found himself in her presence.

Yet, he also felt the softer, more friendship-based feelings he felt for his sisters-in-law. He felt both styles of emotion when in her presence, and this confused him and made him hesitate to either become close friends with her, or drag her to the nearest bed-like piece of furniture and fuck her senseless.

In some respects, this card game was perfect for him. He hoped he could decide through the sharing of small intimacies and confidences whether he wanted a friendship-based relationship with Chloe or a sexually based one.

His mind shied away from a deep enough relationship where they would be both friends *and* lovers. Treading down that path would ultimately only hurt both himself and Chloe, and he had no wish to hurt her. Fuck her 'til they both dropped from sated exhaustion, yes, but hurt her, no.

Samuel realized Chloe had been staring at her particular card for a few minutes now. Lost in his own thoughts as he had been, he hadn't noticed the passing of time.

"What is it? Come on, don't kill me with the suspense."

He watched her shift uncomfortably. She shifted her legs underneath her and finally looked up from the small card.

"Describe one of your favorite fantasies."

Samuel grinned. He had checked with Dominic before he and Mary had left that there wasn't anything *too* personal on the cards. His brother had grinned in that charming manner that used to have women falling at his feet, and declared some of them came close to too personal, but nothing he hadn't been able to handle.

Samuel had grinned back at his brother, determined to pick up the gauntlet that had been thrown down.

Samuel smiled into Chloe's slightly worried eyes, sat back, and closed his own eyes. He tried to clear his mind — to picture a favorite fantasy — but nothing sprang to mind.

He had a zillion fantasies, but he wanted a special one for Chloe. Thinking of her, picturing her naked and waiting for him, a scene began to form in his mind. He spoke aloud as the scene unfolded.

"I'm naked and lying back on something soft. Bed, couch, rug — it doesn't matter what it is. My fantasy woman kisses me, and I hungrily kiss her back, gently biting her soft lips."

With his eyes closed, Samuel could mentally see Chloe kissing him. He could feel himself tasting her soft, full lower lip. He tried not to groan and shifted in his chair.

"She pulls back, and with lots of skin-on-skin contact, she strings kisses down my chest, arrowing downwards." Samuel built the fantasy in his mind. He pictured Chloe kissing her way down his chest, wet kisses, nibbling, taking her time and enjoying the process.

"My fantasy woman takes her time, draws out the moment. I think we're in firelight; I enjoy the glow of the crackling flames shedding light on her brown hair. She nibbles me and kisses me. She works her way down my chest until she reaches my cock."

Pausing for a moment, eyes still closed, Samuel imagined what it would feel like to have Chloe pause for a similar moment as her chin lightly grazed his hugely erect staff.

It would be painful ecstasy. Samuel cracked one eye open, gazed over at Chloe, still sitting with her legs crossed under her. Her eyes were wide and slightly glazed. Obviously she, too, was picturing what his fantasy would be like.

Before he could lose the moment, Samuel re-closed his eyes, delving back into the fantasy that was quickly becoming his favorite.

"She teases me a moment, but not for long. Before I need to guide her with my hand, she lowers her head and takes the whole head of my cock into her mouth. She's warm, wet. I imagine it's her pussy she's taking me into.

"Without real thought, I tilt my hips and try to get more of myself inside her. I can't help it. The soft inner walls of her mouth are so wet and sucking on me. Her tongue flicks out and creates an electric reaction through me. I feel it arc from my toes all the way up through my cock. The tight contractions of her mouth as she sucks me harder drive me wild. I can feel the heat and urgency mount inside me, filling my whole body with the need to draw her closer and ram deep inside her.

"It starts in my balls. I can feel them tighten and rise up in a salute to the woman. But soon the heat and energy course through my iron-hard shaft. Next thing the heat and urgency are in my belly, twisting and causing me to moan, to thrust myself harder and deeper into her. I can't get enough of her wet heat, I feel the urgency grow and grow.

"Thankfully, she relaxes her throat and accepts me, accepts my desires and needs, and embraces me. The strange thing is, the more she accepts and embraces me, the more I want and need her. The more urgently the demands of my body rage.

"I can feel myself climbing up the peak with startling haste. The fire in my balls and stomach rages hotter. I start to pump faster and deeper. I start to cry out, any release to keep the pleasant pressure in my balls intact.

"When my cries hit a certain note, my fantasy woman knows I'm about to explode. She pulls her mouth away from me, and the cold, the loss, the emptiness is like a bucket of ice water. This time I cry out in loss and devastation.

"Before I can do anything, she has straddled me and is plunging her cunt deep, deep down onto me. My back arches with the fiery pleasure. I can barely believe the change from pain and loneliness to warmth and the close embrace in such a blink of an eye.

"I crack my eyes open, to stare at the beautiful creature riding me, taking her own pleasure and giving me so much. She rides me, hard and fast. It's exactly what I need right now. No gentle caresses, no teasing bites. Just hard, raw, deep fucking. Within seconds all the heat and fire is back inside me. My balls are so tight I think they're going to explode. The fiery pain is in my stomach and my cock is as hard as iron. I can feel the beginning trembles, the shakes that indicate I'm about to explode.

"I warn the fantasy woman, I tell her something to indicate I'm about to explode. Just like with her mouth and her body, she embraces my passions, my wild side. She simply keeps on thrusting down on me, over and over, pushing me beyond control and over the edge.

"I come inside her like a geyser. Pumping load after load of my seed inside her, I bathe her insides with my essence. Shouting my joy and grasping her hips to get even deeper inside her, I hold her tightly so she can't move, can't escape me or my passion.

"Coming for a man is intense. It's this huge release of pressure, both in the body and mind. For a moment, after you've shot your seed deep inside your chosen woman, you feel lightheaded and like the king of the world. And then you feel deflated and empty. That's why many men don't mind a bit of cuddling after exploding inside a woman. It lets us regroup. I pull my fantasy woman close to me. Hug her close for the warmth of her skin, massaging her back, smelling the sweet scent of her hair.

"It's only then that I realize my woman didn't come. As I stroke her back and nuzzle her curls, I feel a much more lethargic sort of passion fill me. It's that satisfied sort of passion. Not as urgent, not as primal. Now the most urgent part of my own lust has so kindly been taken care of, it's only fair I return the favor to my magnificent fantasy woman.

"I flip her onto her back and spread her lusciously long legs wide, wide apart. I see that her light brown fur down there is trimmed, but not fully shaven. I *love* a woman who is trimmed. The delicate pink of her clit draws me to her. I bend down and start to lave and suck at her erect clit."

Samuel, now onto the second part of his fantasy, wanted to see Chloe's reaction. He had deliberately described himself coming first, even though he rarely let it happen in reality. He knew when it came to Chloe, she would hold out on the sexual side of their relationship as long as possible. So by the time they finally came around to fucking, more than likely he would be so desperate to come inside her, he wouldn't be able to control himself.

He was not a selfish man, almost always he was more concerned his partner find sexual satisfaction over his own. Yet with Chloe, he knew he would need to get some of his own pent-up lust sated, even in a fantasy, before he could try to seduce Chloe with a clear mind and willing body.

Looking over at the object of his fantasy, he smiled in masculine satisfaction to see her eyes were dilated and a delicate flush had crept up her face as she became more and more involved in his fantasy.

"I lick and suck her to my heart's content, thrusting my fingers inside her. I have three, or maybe even four fingers curved and fluted inside her so they stretch her to capacity. I continue to tease her and pump her until she screams and begs and drags me so close to her core we smash together in that wet, sucking way only oral sex produces. With my face pressed against her clit and my fingers soaked, covered in her juices and the remnants of my own seed, I finally so-gently bite down on her clit. The pain mixed with the pleasure forces her over the brink of climax, and I return my thanks to her for the incredible joy she has given me."

Samuel ran his eyes heatedly over her lithe figure. *How* he wished he could get up, pull her out of the chair and down onto the floor and plunge his aching self into her over and over until they both screamed with the satisfaction.

"With the Goddess' help, my cock is again at full attention by now, and on the tide of her orgasm I can thrust myself so deeply inside her we both ache with the power. I would ride her hard and quickly, so she would have yet another climax directly on top of her oral one, and her sweet body contracting around my hard meat would send me over the edge as well."

Trying to ignore the sweat trickling down the side of his face, and also ignore the fire in his groin, desperate to be put out with this sweet woman, Samuel grinned a large, hungry, purely wolfish grin.

"Then, Goddess willing, we would be able to catch our breaths and start all over again."

Samuel laughed as Chloe's eyes widened, either in disbelief or jealous lust. Or maybe both. Taking a deep breath to calm his racing heart, he placed his leg back onto the floor and bent forward resting his arms on his legs in what he hoped was a casual stance.

"So, darling," he purred, "do share. I've done my part. Describe to me one of your favorite fantasies."

Chapter Eight

ᏠᏉ

Chloe tried to calm her hammering heart. Ignoring the sweat trickling down her back, she swallowed.

If exercise could be defined as one's heart rate accelerating, then she had probably had her week's worth right then. Either Samuel was the best spinner of tales, or he had purposefully done a magnificent job turning her on, simply by describing the hottest, most erotic fantasy she had ever heard.

And now he sat there, appearing totally calm, waiting for her to return the favor. The man obviously had no idea of how hot he made her. The thought rankled, yet conversely made her feel safe at the same time. Besides, she wasn't perfectly sure she *could* return the favor of a similarly hot, sexy fantasy, surely not as well as he had just done for her.

She glanced at the clock, hoping she could put him off while she desperately sought to think of something even half as erotic as his little tale.

She heard him *tut* at her.

"Now, now. No escape for you, little girl. I upheld my end of the deal. I'm breathless with anticipation to hear one of your fantasies. Just sit back, relax, and tell it to me."

Determined not to wimp out, Chloe moved her feet into a more comfortable position underneath her. She leaned back in the overstuffed chair, closed her eyes and let her mind wander at will.

A picture began to form in her head.

She seemed to be in the woods at night—just like the original night she had arrived here. The rich brown of the soil beneath her feet was soft and moist. The grass was a dark, beautifully rich green color. Large, towering trees rose up all around her. The night sky formed a midnight blue blanket around her. Chloe looked around her small fantasy world and realized a huge wolf was padding out of the trees, heading towards her. She recognized him as Samuel.

He halted a few feet from her, and began to shimmer, much as he had that first night. Between one blink and the next, he stands before her, gloriously naked, with the moon shining on his lightly tanned skin. Lean muscles gleaming, huge cock fully erect and drawing her closer to where he stands.

She takes a step closer to him, seemingly drawn by his handsomeness, the electric connection they seemed to share. He also takes a step towards her, bringing them so close together she could lean forward just an inch to rest her head against his strong chest.

Just as her imaginary Samuel reaches an arm out to touch her, caress her, she pulled her mind away from the potent fantasy. Part of her desperately craved to indulge in the fantasy, to let him draw her up into him and kiss her senseless, yet she couldn't indulge herself right now.

Reality was Samuel sitting opposite her in her cousin's cabin, waiting for her to share a fantasy. This particular fantasy, she knew, was one to re-create and wallow in alone with her vibrator long after he had left, not to be spoken aloud and held answerable for.

Pulling her mind up and away from the drugging intensity of that particular fantasy, she opened her eyes, grateful she hadn't become so ensnared in her own fantasy to have spoken it aloud to Samuel.

"You going to tell me that one?" he queried, staring intently at her with a familiar flame burning deeply in his deep blue eyes.

"Uh, no. I think I'll keep that one to myself."

Samuel seemed to think of that for a moment, then nod. "Fair enough. But you better have something good to replace it with. From over here that looked like a mighty fine fantasy."

Chloe smiled, relieved to be let off the hook.

"Well, one of my long-standing fantasies is to do it in the ocean at nighttime. A pool would suffice in a pinch, but the real fantasy is the ocean. I love the wildness one can find in the ocean, and I specified nighttime because something about the night lets me relax and break free for a bit."

Samuel smiled lazily. "Do tell."

Closing her eyes, she thought of the rolling dark ocean on a lovely hot summer's night.

"Imagine being in the ocean on one of those lovely hot, balmy summer evenings. The air is hot, the sun's just set, so the sky still has traces of light, but is that lovely twilight, dark blue color. A few scattered stars are out, only the largest and brightest. I love the ebb and pull of the ocean. I could stand in the waves, the water up to my neck, for hours and just let the ocean push and pull me around. I love the sound of the waves crashing on the sand, loud, but so sweet to one's ears, don't you think?"

Silently, Chloe built the image in her mind. Remembered every beloved vacation as a child, every escape she had made down to the coast. She imagined herself standing in the ocean, warm, but cool at the same time, surrounded by such a mass of water. She could hear the crash of the waves, smell the tangy salt in the air.

"Mmm," Samuel murmured, "I agree there are few things more seductive than standing in the ocean at dusk on a hot summer night. However, I must admit to being more interested in what your fantasy man *does* to you in the ocean."

Chloe smiled and opened her eyes, looking over at the hunk sitting opposite her.

"Why Samuel, what a one-track mind you have. Couldn't my fantasy man and I simply stand next to each other in the ocean, enjoying the ebb and pull of nature's waves? Enjoy the beauty of the night?"

Samuel grinned. The toothy grin reminded her of how he might smile in his wolf form. "I might be able to stand there platonically," he raised an eyebrow at her muffled laugh, "but *you* on the other hand would likely do something to distract me and ruin my good intentions."

Chloe grinned, totally missing the reference to them being together in her fantasy.

"Maybe. Maybe not. Depends on how easy it is to distract you." Sitting back, she smiled at him.

"I suppose I have the same sort of fantasy every women does. I would love to have total, unrestricted access to my man. I wouldn't want to have my hands pushed away with a fierce '*Not here!*' or '*Not now!*' hissed at me. Or worse, to be grudgingly allowed to tease and feel my way around and be stoically put up with. Just like men want women who are open and honest with their feelings, so do women want to be embraced and allowed to explore their own desires. I think one of the biggest factors turning women off exploring their men is the fear they'll be turned away or told they're doing it wrong."

Samuel raised an eyebrow in total disbelief. Chloe frowned.

"Don't look like that. I'm serious. I've dated a couple of guys who were far more interested in their image than in exploring the more sexual side to a relationship. Guys like that really are out there. Believe it or not, just like there are women with high and low sex drives—so too are there men around who simply have more important things on their minds than sex."

Samuel thought about her words, and then grudgingly nodded. "Now that I think about it, I agree with you. It's just not something one comes across regularly in a man."

Chloe nodded. "True. But having been with a few men who had a different sex drive to mine, that sort of compatibility isn't something I take for granted anymore."

Samuel grinned. "With the right man, sexual compatibility won't be an issue, I can guarantee it."

Chloe smiled, more than certain Samuel's sexual drive was a match for her own. "I believe you."

"Do go on, little girl. You hold me breathless with anticipation."

Chloe raised an eyebrow.

"After all the luscious details I gave you about myself and my fantasy woman, I would dare to say you owe me a deeper description of this fantasy man you explore in the ocean."

Chloe smiled and went back to her fantasy.

"When my fantasy man and I are in the ocean, I'd love to softly feel the muscles in his legs, work my way up massaging his calves and thighs. I'd love to fondle his cock, feel him grow iron-hard in my hand despite the chill in the ocean. I'd enjoy staring up at the sky as it grew darker, watch the stars begin to shine, and then look back in his face and see his passion and impatience grow.

"I'd love to bring him along, step-by-step, and maybe even make him come without laying my lips on him to begin with. The power of knowing I could bring him to climax by neither kissing him nor sucking on him, but just with my hand. Oh, I'd love to do all that later, spread out on a large towel with no one around. But part of the fantasy is to feel that momentary power, knowing I could bring my man to climax with just my hands. I would wallow in the knowledge that he wanted me and lusted after me that much, it would give me the confidence in return to follow and fulfill all his own fantasies."

Chloe let her mind wander over how lovely the fantasy would be, let it play out in her mind, keeping silent, assuming the visuals she had built would be enough for Samuel to use his own imagination.

Samuel looked slightly crestfallen. "That's it? You're leaving me hanging here?"

Chloe smiled and shook her head. "Obviously I'm going to have to spell it out. I forgot men have less imagination than women."

Samuel looked a bit put out. He pouted, but ruined it by the grin that shone through.

Chloe shook her head. "You big baby. Okay, let me spell it out for you in minute detail."

He shone a happy grin over her, settled himself in his chair and closed his eyes, obviously looking forward to her words.

"Imagine you're standing in the ocean. Your feet are braced apart, to keep you upright as the waves gently pull you back and forth. The ebb and flow of the water is so subtle, you don't really notice it or think of it. Yet at the same time, it is powerful enough that you must dig your feet into the sand and use a lot of your strength to keep from being knocked over.

"That subtlety, that powerful, strong-yet-still-subtle movement is more of what I'm talking about. Imagine having the hot night air around you, and the cool but still warm water surrounding your body, and having female flesh pressed up against you. Say you're holding her, arms wrapped around her waist. She slowly starts caressing your thigh. Such a small, light caress you barely even notice it. Just like the pull in the water, it is gentle, soft, barely noticeable. Until you suddenly realize your cock is half-hard."

Chloe looked at Samuel and realized he had opened his eyes to watch her as she described her fantasy. His gaze was hot as he became more ensnared in her descriptions, as they lost themselves in her fantasy. Men, she knew, were more visual creatures. So while she could use her own imagination to fill in the blanks of her own fantasy, she realized she needed to describe her thoughts into words to let him get the full impact of what she was trying to convey.

"Her light, gentle massaging is merely building the fire inside your groin, not putting it out. After a few minutes, not even the cool chill in the water can dampen the sexual arousal. Yet you can't make her work faster, or stroke harder. She is gently caressing your thighs, working her way up. Soon she will reach your cock. Yet she won't dip her hand into your trunks, she will simply massage you through the Lycra.

"You're starting to breathe harder, the fire in your cock is getting hotter. Your lover is still massaging you, gently caressing you, but the hunger, the arousal and ache inside you is growing stronger. Her caresses aren't relieving the stress. You're in the ocean, maybe the odd person now and then walks by you on the beach, calling out 'Good evening' so you can't pick her up and fuck her wildly on the beach. You have to stand and take her explorations."

Chloe enjoyed dragging the fantasy out, fleshing out more and more details to drive her point home to Samuel. The way he shifted on his chair showed his jeans were obviously becoming too tight.

"So maybe instead, you growl at her to hurry up and fist you. She smiles up at you, and reminds you that you promised her she could take her time, explore you in the relative safety of the ocean. You can't go back on your word, of course. So you must stand there, with the waves ebbing and pulling at you, a beautiful woman in your arms slowly driving you wild, and the odd night stroller walking down the sand. You can't take her, you simply have to let her sate her curiosity. I'd be willing to bet her exploring you would quickly drive you insane."

Smiling in a slightly smug manner, Chloe leaned forward, balanced on her legs.

"So, Samuel, think it's a tame fantasy of mine now?"

He swallowed, stunned for a moment. With obvious effort he collected himself, swallowing a few more times, until the fire in his eyes became banked. "It's definitely worth a thought or two. Except there is one point you missed."

Chloe frowned. "It's my fantasy, I can't have missed anything."

"Sure you could have. If that man *was* me, and the woman driving him wild was you, then I would have had a simple solution when I truly couldn't take any more."

Chloe raised an eyebrow arrogantly. "Oh?"

"Yeah," he drawled. "I would have ripped off those tiny bikini panties, stripped out of my own trunks, and driven myself so far inside you your screams would echo across the beach."

Chloe swallowed, easily picturing in her mind Samuel doing just that. It certainly had a devastating effect on her heartbeat.

"Well, that is one solution. I hadn't quite gotten that far in the fantasy, but your input is noted and will be attended to later. I was thinking more along the lines of teasing you until you came under the water. I'm sure it would be a novel experience for most men."

Samuel stood up. "I'd much rather the novel experience of coming inside you, little girl."

Frowning, Chloe stood up. "I'm not sure—"

Samuel leaned forward and pressed one finger across her lips, silencing her.

"Let's not go there tonight. It's late now. What say you come over to my cabin for dinner tomorrow? We can go on a dusk walk, work up an appetite and I'll cook you some dinner. We can move onto the medium cards, the ones with green borders."

Chloe looked at the box of cards. She certainly had no intention of chickening out now. She had survived tonight intact, heart-whole and with a strong sense of self-confidence she had never really felt around this man.

Sure, she was horny as hell and relieved she had the forethought to pack spare batteries for her vibrator, but she hadn't cast herself at his feet begging to be fucked. One must look on the bright side here.

Maybe she had blown the whole situation out of proportion in her mind. Being with Samuel and keeping her heart away from him hadn't been quite as hard as she had feared.

"Okay. I'll probably be itching for a walk by then anyway."

"Head on over anytime after five. We can go for another walk down into the forest."

Nodding, Chloe stood up and followed him to the door. She held herself still when he bent down to give her a kiss.

Even the chaste goodbye kiss made her toes curl, made the hair on her nape stand up. She resisted the impulse to touch her lips when his finally left hers. With a wave and a quick backward glance, Samuel was quickly swallowed up by the night. Chloe shut and locked the door, wondering at the wisdom of a short-term fling with the man.

It had been far too long since she had indulged in anything other than her vibrator. A real flesh-and-blood man in her bed would be a welcome change. Yet she was wary, as Mary had insisted on having only one night with Dominic. They had somehow fallen in love during that one night. Even though they were very happily married, Chloe had always wanted to retain her independence, something that too often disappeared when one became heavily involved with a man.

The thought of falling in love with a man like Samuel, the most confirmed bachelor probably in the entire state, was a scary proposition. Men like Samuel Rutledge did not fall in love; they had lustful affairs and then moved on, leaving a trail of broken hearts.

Yet what harm could a few nights do? The little demon in her head whispered. She lived on the other end of the state; she had her own home, her own life, far, far away from here. It wasn't as if a few nights of incredible sex would shatter her heart, she tried to convince herself. She was a big girl now.

Showering and changing into the old T-shirt and flannel pajama pants she slept in, Chloe mulled over the pros and cons of sleeping with Samuel.

As she lay her head down on the pillow, still wrestling with her desires, she finally decided to go for it. It wasn't as if the man could cast a spell over her, or ensnare her and bind her to him with pure sex alone. She would never live with, or marry a man who wasn't one hundred percent devoted to her and in love with her.

As there was little doubt Samuel would ever be either of those, then there wasn't really any risk, was there?

The silence in her head might have worried her if she hadn't been so tired. Her little voices weren't arguing with her, yet, nor were they agreeing with her. Chloe's physical cravings had finally silenced them all.

Chloe slept dreamlessly yet again.

Chapter Nine
Saturday Morning

☙

Chloe sat in the dirt in her oldest paint-stained pair of jeans and a torn T-shirt. Digging in Mary's woefully unkempt vegetable patch, she happily weeded as she thought.

The two main issues buzzing in her head were vastly different, yet both were knotty problems and seemed incredibly hard to work through.

For the moment, however, she was ignoring her decision to seduce Samuel tonight. Instead, she was trying to figure out what she wanted to do with her life, where she wanted to head. Not quite the same squirm-worthy thoughts, but she reminded herself the whole reason for her wanting the peaceful solitude of the cabin was to work out what she wanted for the next few years in her life.

Talking to the vegetables as she fiercely pulled weeds was proving far more soothing and helpful than driving around the too well-known local blocks, or sitting back at home on her bed or in her favorite chair, mulling over her options had ever been.

"Stop procrastinating girl, and work this out," she muttered as she pulled yet another weed out and placed it on the heap that soon would be transferred to the compost pile.

"Teaching had been fun," she acknowledged to herself and the scattered vegetables, "but it was only subbing, so even then I still simply played at it. The real question is, do I want to spend years and years getting my degree? It would be better to try teaching younger kids, maybe even the elementary classes, but I'd still require official training even in that."

Mulling this over and weighing the pleasure the thought brought her, she nodded her head. As she often did while alone and contemplating deeply, she began to talk to herself.

"Yeah, teaching brought me a lot of satisfaction. Maybe I should look into subbing in the local elementary school back home or something. There's always room for a substitute somewhere in elementary schools, those kids transfer sickness like the plague. Also a bonus for me, it's not like I could get bored with changing classes all the time, and it's something I can start as soon as I head back, subbing doesn't require a degree or anything."

Weeding now with a vengeance, Chloe thought through her decision. She had a feeling that teaching kids, helping them grow and develop would soon prove to be a passion of the heart.

She had performed so many jobs it would be fairly easy to give a personal account to the kids of all the different styles of jobs one could take and roughly what they all involved. Guiding the next generation of workers might be fulfilling indeed.

Chloe found herself smiling. The more she thought about becoming a "real" teacher, instead of simply playing at it for a six month stint for a friend who had the gall to tromp off to Europe for a term, the happier she became. As usual, she smiled at the irony of simply falling into a job. That's always how it seemed to occur for her.

A long time later she stood up to stretch the kinks out of her legs. Vainly trying to brush some of the dirt from her jeans, she surveyed her hard work. There was nothing like weeding a desperately needy garden to clear the mind.

Chloe smiled in satisfaction, both of the newly weeded garden, as well as her new direction in life.

Now she just had to resolve the small issue of major sexual tension between herself and Samuel. Her plans to seduce him tonight would relieve some of that stress. While she wasn't stupid enough to think one night would be enough, with luck having a brief affair would work. She was only staying for a few more days—she would have to make the most of their time together before she went back home and began her newly found career as a substitute teacher.

Chapter Ten
Dusk that night

ɞ

Samuel was startled to find himself restlessly pacing up and down his living room. Having dutifully given his small cabin a quick cleaning, showering and dressing in jeans and a casual shirt, he had moved to the living room for a soothing drink of scotch.

Having taken a sip and replacing the glass, he had finally let his thoughts take over.

To seduce, or to not seduce.

This dilemma had been the main topic of conversation in his head since heading off late last night into the dark woods, leaving behind the object of his lusts and fantasies.

His hard-on, which he had been wearing for the better part of two days now, was eagerly interested in the seduction. *Any* seduction as long as it resulted in thrusting itself to the hilt in the so-sweet Chloe.

His confirmed bachelor ways, however, were firmly pointing out the downside to seducing a virtual member of his family. If he were to seduce her, fuck her senseless, then find himself growing bored with her, as so often happened, then Dominic, not to mention Mary, would likely want to kill him and the very first Rutledge shotgun wedding in history would occur.

And so his brain tried to act as umpire between the two warring parts of him. His cock was desperate, yet for the first time he could ever recall since trying to decide between the luscious Cindy and the devastatingly gorgeous Trudy when losing his virginity, he hesitated.

What if he grew tired of Chloe within the week, as usually happened? How could he let her down easy? What was worse was the nagging, constantly squashed worry, what would he do if he *didn't* grow tired of her.

What if he set out the ground rules, insisted on only a few nights of fantastic, mind-blowing sex, and then he realized he wanted more.

Samuel halted as he found himself pacing yet again.

He cringed with the realization no woman had *ever* had him pacing so restlessly, not even his sisters-in-law. They often had him wanting to run wild or smash his fist into a wall, but no woman he could recall had ever had him pacing a hole in the floor.

Just as he resumed his pacing, driven nuts by the thoughts in his head and the wicked fantasies his cock obviously reveled in, the door knocker sounded.

Muttering a curse and adjusting his jeans in the vain hope Chloe wouldn't notice the bulging hard-on he wore, he crossed over to let his guest in.

He opened the door and vaguely felt his mouth fall open. Chloe stood on his doorstep in the tightest pair of dark blue jeans he had ever seen. They molded her long, *very* long legs, showing the nicely toned flesh encased within. Certainly not model-slim, as his women usually were, but the sheer length of the legs she showed had him drooling like a pup.

A short-sleeved silk shirt fluttered in the slight breeze, hinting at the luscious breasts he just *knew* were waiting beneath.

A handful, his brain registered, *definitely a handful*.

Snapping his mouth shut, Samuel grinned. It looked to him as if little Chloe had decided for them both how the evening would progress.

Fantastic. If she's made the decision to seduce me, then I can certainly return the favor and seduce her!

"Good evening, Chloe. You look fantastic."

For the first time *ever,* he felt his legs wobble oh-so-slightly as she grinned up at him. She looked him over, head to foot, in a manner he was more than used to from women, just not from *her.*

"Good evening, Samuel. You're looking in mighty fine form tonight yourself."

This was directed down around his cock-level, and his already painful shaft simply swelled and grew with the praise. He tried not to wince at the pain the restraining jeans caused him. When Chloe's knowing grin brightened even more, he wasn't certain he had hidden the wince perfectly.

Stepping back, hoping to readjust the pressure in his jeans, he waved her inside his cabin.

"Please come in. Let's skip the walk. Dinner will be ready in a minute, and the game is waiting."

Chloe entered the door, brushing herself up against him as she came forward to plant a small kiss on his cheek.

Damn, he thought, dazed, *she's using my own tricks back on me*!

Feeling a grudging respect for the woman, he acknowledged she was certainly a woman on the hunt tonight.

He grinned as he followed the deliciously feminine, totally bite-able, female swaying ass into the living room.

He loved a challenge.

Chapter Eleven

Chloe swallowed the brief flare of panic she felt at the heated lust raging in Samuel's eyes. She sincerely hoped she wasn't playing with the proverbial fire. A girl would have to be blind not to notice the stupendously erect cock inside his jeans, and from the look of wild lust shining in his eyes, Samuel was more than ready to explode at any given second.

The scent of tomatoes and meaty pasta wafted into the small living room from the kitchen. The normal, delicious scent helped her regain her equilibrium, and gather her nerves tightly under control. Sniffing appreciatively, she smiled as she turned back to her host, nerves fully under control.

"That smells delicious. I didn't realize you could cook."

Even though the grin Samuel gave her was half-hearted, it still took her breath away. *Damn the man for being so sexy, I can't keep on losing my mind every time he looks at me.*

"Gramps made sure all four of us could cook. Insisted it was a life skill. That's my infamous lasagna you smell. A rare treat indeed."

Chloe smiled. "Well, I am truly appreciative. Let's eat while we play, hmm?"

She slowly followed him into the small kitchen, prepared to help out in any way. She noticed the two dinner plates already set out with salads, and stood back to watch as Samuel put on oven mitts and withdrew a huge dish of lasagna from the oven. A flick of his wrist turned the gas off, and Chloe stared at the enormous dish.

"I really hope you're eating most of that. It looks fantastic, but it would take me over a week to get through even half of that."

Samuel chuckled. "I always make twice as much lasagna as I need. The kids always come over for leftovers—they can scent my lasagna from a mile away—and I, myself, enjoy eating it cold for breakfast or lunch the following day."

Nodding, Chloe watched as he expertly sliced two large portions, and took the plate he offered her. With cutlery and napkins, she followed him back into the living room where a coffee table had been drawn up with the box of cards sitting in its middle.

She took her seat next to him on the couch, at the other end so they both had room to spread out a little and start their lasagna.

Chloe blew on it a moment, enjoying the fresh, steamy pasta smell. So very fresh from the oven, she knew intellectually it was too hot to eat, but it smelled too good to wait around for.

Blowing as daintily as she could onto the piece on her fork, she finally decided to risk burning her mouth and she took her first bite. Without even meaning to, she closed her eyes in ecstasy as the meat, tomato and parmesan mixed and melted on her tongue.

It was delicious! The pasta was soft but not limp, the tomato sauce accentuated the meaty bolognaise making it seem more hearty and richer. Cheese had been liberally strewn over the top and throughout the meaty sauce so it dripped over the side of the slice and meshed with her salad.

Altogether it was a decadent, delicious slice of lasagna, the best she had ever tasted.

Chloe swiped her tongue out to catch the parmesan as it threatened to drip out of her mouth. Picking up a fresh roll from the basket Samuel had carried over with him from the kitchen, she dunked it unceremoniously into the meaty sauce oozing out the side of her slice of lasagna.

Either Samuel had been given help, or he was the best lasagna maker she had ever met. Considering his pride in the dish, she felt it a fair bet to think he had made it from scratch himself.

After a number of mouthfuls, she managed, "This is fantastic. Is the recipe a family secret, or can you teach me it later?"

Samuel smiled. "It's not exactly a secret, but it's not written down, either. I can jot it down for you and try to show you another time."

That said, they both dug back into their respective plates. All too soon she was full to bursting and had to sit back, placing her hand on her belly.

"If I eat another bite I'm going to explode, but it's just so good I'm not sure I can help myself!"

Samuel was mopping up the last of his meat sauce with a crust of bread. He glanced up with a smile.

"I'll take that as a compliment."

"Oh, do! It was fantastic. I really want to eat more—but I'll never be able to move again."

Samuel swiped at the last of his sauce, and popped the crust into his mouth, chewing on it. Gallantly, he picked up her plate and, along with his own, carried them through into the kitchen where she heard the water running.

"Leave the dishes," she called out. "I'll do them after we let this meal settle down."

In an instant she heard the water shut off. He came back through the door.

"Now there's an offer I can't refuse. I just wanted to rinse them before the sauce dries on the plates. Personally, I hate doing dishes."

Chloe grinned. "I don't mind cooking, but I don't do it too often anymore, living alone. I usually prefer washing up after a really good meal. I just don't think I'm capable of moving yet."

Samuel grinned and sat on the opposite end of the couch. Bending forward, he brought the box of cards over to the edge of the table, so they both could reach into it easily. Chloe made herself comfortable, half turned towards Samuel on the couch.

"Shall we start, little girl? Now that we've both been fed, we can concentrate on other matters rather than our empty bellies."

The grin he shot her was huge and sexy. "Ladies first," he insisted, offering her the box of cards as if it were the Holy Grail, or Pandora's box of sin and temptation.

Shooting him a cheeky grin, she smiled brightly. "Why, thank you, kind sir."

Being careful to select a green-edged card, she withdrew one at random and eagerly sat back to see how the evening would begin.

Chapter Twelve

ରେ

Samuel watched with growing lust and uncertainty as Chloe read and then reread her card. She seemed faintly shocked, but he could scent her lust and desire seeping from her very pores.

She smelled delicious to him. Fresh as the wind, yet with the faintly flowery, feminine scent that was sweet and uniquely hers. Overriding all these scents was the salty tang of her lust and cream.

He *so* wanted to spread her legs and taste her. It was a burning in his gut, an ache in his loins, and the fiercest craving he'd ever had, all wrapped up into the one package.

The pause dragged out until he could feel the pulse beat in his head and echo down in his cock. If she didn't talk soon he'd go mad, he knew. After an eternity of lustful waiting, she cleared her throat.

"Uh, I'm not sure we can do this one — do you have shot glasses?"

Samuel blinked, startled and slightly confused. "Well, yeah. Why?"

Chloe finally raised her eyes and looked at them. A vortex of emotions swirled therein. He could read lust, excitement and a sparkle of mischief within her dark, deep brown eyes. He felt certain if he stared in their depths long enough he would be able to read her soul.

Without a single word, but with a mischievous, almost impish grin on her face she bent forward, her legs grazing his own much larger ones, and she handed him the small card she held.

He must drink a shot from between her breasts.

That single, oh-so-simple sentence had his cock so hard and long he feared he would come in his pants. Never, in all his life had he come in his pants. The images, the simple words and the erotic pictures they conjured in his head had his cock fit to bursting.

At this rate he would spew his seed far and wide before even entering Chloe's lush heat. With an iron will, he pulled his thoughts away from sinking himself balls-deep into Chloe and stood up.

Silently commending himself for his strength of will, he muttered something vaguely along the lines of, "I'll get the glasses", and headed off into the kitchen. He needed the moment to splash cold water on his face and regroup anyway.

Pulling his jeans away from his engorged cock, he dared not touch himself for fear he would explode under the pressure.

"Don't forget something to drink," Chloe called out from the next room.

Picking up a bottle of vodka from his highest shelf — where much younger, busy and eager little hands couldn't reach it — he snagged two shot glasses and headed back, determined to keep his control until Chloe was in the same state as himself.

Returning to the living room, sitting down on the edge of the couch, Samuel watched with undisguised desire as Chloe unbuttoned the top of her shirt. She bent forward to the table and poured half a glass full of the vodka, then carefully arranged the shot glass within her cleavage.

Grinning, she gingerly withdrew her hands, slowly, to make sure the glass was firmly entrenched between her beautiful breasts. The silk shirt still hid most of the mounds from his view, but the healthy show of cleavage was all his poor system could currently cope with.

If he could see any more of her silky smooth skin, if her scent was any further in his system, he would pull her down, tear the clothes from her sweet body and fuck her wildly until they both screamed and collapsed from exhaustion.

"Okay, you can go for it now, just be careful not to spill too much. I have a feeling spilled vodka on skin will become rather sticky."

Nodding curtly, not trusting his voice to do anything but growl in sexual hunger, he held her waist steady. His hand easily cupped the rounded flesh, the sensation of palming her skin, even through the thin fabric of her shirt, had him incoherent in his lust.

He dipped his head, determined to drink the shot of vodka and leave her be.

His head bent down, angling between her breasts and he inhaled a pure shot of her scent. It invaded his system like a drug, made him higher than any steroid or amphetamine ever could. He closed his eyes, certain the color in the world just got that much brighter, that much more vivid.

Riding the wave of lust and painful pleasure, Samuel took a moment to gather himself.

Thrusting his tongue in an imitation of what his penis desperately wanted to do, he lapped at the vodka between her perfect breasts.

It was on his second foray he realized she wasn't wearing a bra. Both her hesitancy, and her unwillingness to remove her shirt became clear. The knowledge that she was naked under the shirt had his cock hardening even more.

A dozen more laps and Samuel sat back. The vodka ran through his system, energizing him and making him even more lightheaded. Or maybe that was still her scent driving him wild.

Blinking, trying to clear his head, he poured the other shot glass half-full of vodka. Offering it to her, he insisted.

"It's better we stay on an equal footing if we're to be drinking. No chance of one of us taking advantage of the other that way."

Removing the shot glass from between her breasts, Chloe smiled and left her shirt half-unbuttoned. As she swapped her empty glass for the full one he offered, she grinned. The shirt gaped, showing a slice of her delicious breasts.

"Sounds fair to me."

With one smooth motion she poured the shot down her throat, swallowing the fiery liquid. Samuel gulped, imagining her swallowing his own seed with much the same casualness.

Carefully placing the shot glass on the table, he picked up a new green-edged card and sat back on the couch.

He hoped to hell "*Fuck madly until you are both exhausted*" was an option sometime soon, or he was likely to be a candidate for the funny farm before the night was out.

Chapter Thirteen

ഇ

Chloe felt the burn of the vodka slide down her throat. She wasn't a huge fan of the liquid, but there were much worse things to drink. She didn't think there'd be much drinking going on through the night anyway. Samuel already looked drunk on lust—with luck she could make a move sooner or later and they could release some of the sexual tension crackling in the air.

She watched Samuel's reaction to the new card. He seemed to think for a few moments, then smile, a very male, self-satisfied smile. He stood up, and walked into the kitchen, saying, "I'll just be a second," over his shoulder.

She sat back, curled her legs up underneath her. She pondered for a moment what his card might say. She heard the fridge door open and close, and his rattling around in cupboards.

Growing more and more intrigued, Chloe twisted around, hoping to catch a glimpse of the man in the kitchen. Not seeing anything through the small door, she turned back around.

A minute later she heard Samuel crossing back to the couch. He held a banana in his hand.

A banana?

Chloe resolved if she was to stick it anywhere near her body she would refuse. A girl had to draw the line somewhere.

He handed it to her and she looked suspiciously from it to the man.

"Eat that," he commanded softly.

Eat it? Her brain echoed stupidly. After that huge supper? Ahhh...eat it and turn him on, be suggestive, she realized. She swallowed a giggle. This should be fun.

She snuggled into the couch cushions and watched Samuel. She expected him to sit back down, but he simply stood in front of her, almost vibrating with intensity.

"Go on, sit down, Samuel. I'll make a little show of this for you."

He stayed there a moment, clearly undecided, then nodded and sat back on the other end of the couch.

Chloe smiled and licked her lips, wetting them for the coming entertainment. She was a tad nervous, but really, it felt a little like "Truth or Dare". How hard could it be to turn on an already impressively turned-on man? A little nibble and wiggle of the eyebrows and maybe he'd even be coming in his pants.

Chloe smiled at her strange thoughts.

This should be lots of fun.

Chapter Fourteen

෩

Samuel watched his vixen lick her lips in anticipation. Was she simply wetting her mouth for the coming show, or was she already trying to drive him wild? Not that it mattered either way, he had been hard for nearly two days now — *anything* she did turned him on.

He fidgeted on the couch. His cock was being truly unruly and making his life miserable. With every twitch, every move, his cock pained him, reminded him how much he wanted this woman. He simply *had* to have her and damn the consequences. All he needed now was a break, an excuse, *any* reason to kiss her over and over again.

He watched, like a man in a trance, as her delicate fingers slowly broke open the skin of the banana. The soft cracking sound echoed through his head. All of his senses were heightened in his lust-crazed state. He could hear the faint tearing of the skin as she peeled it down the flesh of the fruit.

Samuel imagined her clothes would make a similar tearing sound as he shredded them from her body, revealing her soft satin skin to his eyes and mouth. Much like Chloe peeling the skin from the fruit revealed its soft flesh to her eyes and mouth.

Slowly, slowly, slowly she peeled the skin down, until finally the fruit was bared to her. Samuel licked his own lips, finding his mouth dry with anticipation.

For a minute, and then two, she turned the naked fruit this way and that, looking at it from all angles. Samuel could feel his heart pounding in his chest. Would she simply take a bite and ruin the fruit? Crushing it under her sharp little teeth?

Or would she treat it with the respect and reverence it deserved?

Samuel shook his head. This was a banana, not his cock. The difference seemed blurred in his ultra-heightened state.

Second by second he felt the moment drag on, until *finally* she opened her mouth wide, jaws unlocking as far as they could, and with her teeth still protected by her soft, soft lips, Chloe lowered her mouth over the banana, closing her lips gently yet firmly over the fleshy fruit.

She held there a minute, and Samuel could feel his heart trying to pound through his chest. His blood raced through his veins, his breath came in short, sharp pants. Oh he was a goner. He craved the feel of those soft lips around his shaft, sucking gently as he could see her cheeks cave in from the suction she was giving that lucky banana.

He felt his face flush, whether in arousal or annoyance he couldn't say. Annoyance that she was lavishing such affection and attention to a stupid piece of fruit, yet the arousal coursing through his system was a heady thing.

If she could give such pleasure to a piece of fruit, the pleasure she could give his cock would be astronomical.

His cock twitched in fierce agreement. Samuel could swear he felt a tiny pearl of seed spurt from his cock. He swallowed, mentally protecting himself for the sights to come.

So very slowly, Chloe raised her head, showing an inch, then two of the banana as she lifted her mouth, caressing the fruit all the way. Samuel swallowed. As a form of self-inflicted torture, there was nothing better.

He felt a lump form in his throat as she lifted her head, then swiped her tongue out to caress the fruit. Samuel felt sweat break out on his forehead.

Then fiercely, she opened her lips again and plunged her mouth back down the fruit.

Samuel gulped, imagining that silky smooth mouth plunging down around his cock. He would fist her hair in his hand, pull her closer, so she was as deeply embedded on his cock as possible, mouth, ass, cunt, anywhere and everywhere.

For the next few minutes, Samuel watched in awe, lust, and jealousy as Chloe gave head to the fucking banana. He wished with a painful desperation that it was his own massive staff receiving the attention.

Not that he could blame anyone but himself. *He* had insisted on playing this stupid game, *he* was the one who had gone off to get the banana instead of taking another card claiming he had none to perform the dare on.

Samuel sighed in frustration.

He was a complete moron.

Finally, driven completely bananas—he nearly howled at the pun, even his mind was against him—he leaned forward and grabbed the stupid piece of fruit from between her lips.

"Stop it! You'll drive me insane."

He grabbed the piece of fruit, wincing as Chloe closed her teeth over the end, tearing its tip off.

She smiled wickedly, chewing the tasty fruit. Samuel looked down at the now mangled phallus object and muttered a foul curse under his breath.

Standing up, adjusting his jeans, totally uncaring of Chloe sitting beside him, he stalked over to the kitchen and happily threw the offensive fruit away in the trash.

He stormed back into the living room and threw himself down on the couch, facing the woman who was driving him nuts.

She was happily chewing on the banana tip. She swallowed and grinned. "I hadn't finished that."

"You're more than finished, woman. Go get the next card before I really lose my temper."

Chloe clucked her tongue. "For someone who initiated this game, you're an awfully sore loser."

"Just get the card, Chloe, or we won't be *playing* anymore."

Putting a strong emphasis on the word "playing", indicating how close to the breaking point he really was, he watched Chloe weigh her options. For a second, he hoped she would make the first move. After teasing him with that damned banana, he was in just the mood to wrestle with her, winning, for once, and then plunging his aching meat deep, deep inside her.

Luckily, or maybe unfortunately, after looking at him very carefully, she nodded once and bent forward to get another card.

Samuel sighed and wondered how long he could play the gentleman before his inner beast broke free and he simply bent her over the nearest surface and fucked her madly.

If the ache in his jeans could be taken as an indication, it wouldn't be much longer.

Chapter Fifteen

** හ**

Chloe read the card and tried to suppress her gleeful look. Samuel was fit to bursting, and with luck this would push him right over the edge.

Okay, so maybe she had gone a little far with the banana. But she didn't want some tepid listless fucking from Samuel. He probably gave that to every other woman he came across. She wanted raw, fierce, primal loving. She wanted everything he had to give her, and maybe even a little more.

And so, she had resolved to push him to his absolute limit, to break his restraint. If she was only having a short time with him, she wanted it to be the absolute best it could be.

And here was her chance.

Determine her bra size.

There was only a handful—she snickered at the pun—of ways for a man to ascertain a lady's bra size, and if she played her cards just right, they could end up determining far more than her 36-C status.

She carefully placed the card on the coffee table, face down, so she could drag out the moment.

Samuel eyed her warily, probably wondering what she was up to. She smiled and leaned back, thrusting her breasts up through the thin silk shirt.

Tilting her head to one side, she smiled seductively. "I hope you can ad lib, Samuel darling," she purred, "because this is a good chance for you to answer some other questions you might have."

He raised his eyebrow and looked *very* interested in what she had to say. "Do tell, vixen."

Chloe smiled. "On the surface, it's a very simple request. But I think we can both make the best of it. You, dear boy, must determine my bra size."

Chloe watched his eyes narrow and hone in on her pert, definitely eager breasts. She could feel her nipples erect and scratch against the material of her shirt. For one very long minute they both sat there—Chloe waiting expectantly, Samuel gazing at her breasts.

Then, very, very slowly, he leaned forward.

Chloe sat still, eagerly waiting for Samuel to make his move. He paused above her, hands hovering within reach, but neither of them touching the ultra-sensitive tips of her breasts.

Samuel reached out one hand and undid the next button of her shirt. With a healthy amount of cleavage now exposed, Chloe found her breath accelerating.

Samuel bent his head, and through the thin silk, he took a mouthful of her breast. Wet heat encased her breast and Chloe found her back arching. Even through her shirt, she could feel the intense heat of his mouth, could feel the dampness seep through the silk.

She moaned at the hot sensations. Samuel sucked her breast, releasing some of the flesh but concentrating on her nipple. Chloe felt her nipple tighten and draw up even more as her back arched her breasts further up into his mouth.

Chloe pressed into him, desperate for more of his heat. She felt Samuel reach around her back, to support her and pull her closer into his embrace. The other hand slid inside her shirt to palm her other breast.

As Samuel sucked and sucked on her breast, Chloe felt her control snap. She needed to feel this man, needed more of his hot flesh for her to touch. She began to fumble with the belt of his jeans.

Without even bothering to lift his head from her breast, Samuel let go of her other breast and quickly tore her shirt apart. Lifting his head only long enough to remove the silk from around her chest, he bared her to his view and lowered his mouth back to her naked breast.

Chloe cried out. Her breasts were so sensitive it was unbelievable. She had thought his mouth hot through the silk of her blouse. Unprotected, his mouth was like a furnace. The pressure from his sucking sent electric shocks from her nipple through to her clit and down to her pulsing pussy.

Samuel sucked and sucked and as the pressure inside her increased and the minutes passed, Chloe felt her brain shattering. Screaming, she came, totally shocked.

Blinking and trying to catch her breath, Chloe looked up at Samuel. His face was flushed a deep red from his restraint, his breath was coming as fast as her own.

"Did I…? Did you…?" Chloe cleared her throat, trying to string a coherent sentence together.

A smug smile blossomed across his face. "Yeah, you did. Let's do it again."

Chloe smiled and started unbuckling his jeans again before he could distract her. Finally pulling the belt free, she unsnapped them, enjoying the feel of the silk boxers he wore.

He groaned as she pushed the thick material down his legs, and lifted himself up onto his arms so she could clear the jeans from his legs.

Grateful he wasn't wearing shoes in the house to slow her down, she eyed the impressive length of leg and tight, taut buns showing through his boxers.

Before she could come back to dip her hands inside the silk boxers, he was tearing her own jeans from her body. Obviously in a rush, he pulled first one leg out, then the other. Chloe chuckled as he struggled to remove her shoes through the jeans.

"I'm not going anywhere, you don't have to rush like this."

"I don't know about you, but I've been wearing my hard-on for more than two days. Time and restraint are not things I have in vast quantities right now."

Chloe lay back down on the couch and let him strip her jeans from her.

"Well then, what are you waiting for? I'm already as wet as I can be."

Samuel finally freed her legs and tossed the jeans casually aside.

"Ah darlin', you ain't seen nothin' yet. I'm gonna make you so wet you'll worry about dehydration."

With that, he easily picked her up and headed off for his bedroom.

Chapter Sixteen

Samuel carefully deposited Chloe on his large bed. In nothing but a skimpy pair of blue panties, she looked luscious and willing. Exactly how he liked his women. In the back of his mind, he knew this was special, knew there was something more going on here. But he refused to think about it. He didn't want to spoil the moment.

He would be forever grateful she arrived tonight dressed for seduction, as he wasn't sure his noble gesture would have lasted through the night. Thankfully, neither would ever really know.

Stripping out of his boxers and pulling his shirt over his head, a split second later he joined Chloe down on his bed. She opened her arms to receive him and he felt like he finally had come home. Kissing her, he slid his tongue inside her mouth. Lapping her, he enjoyed her unique taste.

Keeping control of himself, Samuel stroked his hands up and down her arms, her sides. Trying desperately hard to go slow, he sensitized Chloe's skin, hoping to steam her up just like he was, and about to explode.

He pulled his mouth from her, began to string nibbling kisses down her neck. So engrossed in keeping his restraint, he was shocked when Chloe grabbed his head and lowered him.

"What are you doing?" he growled against her skin.

"You're going too slow. I thought you were a man of action."

"Trying not to rush you," he muttered.

When Chloe pulled her panties off and spread her legs wide, he nearly swallowed his tongue.

"Trust me, Sam, I don't need slow right now. I need a good, hard fuck. Taste me, see how wet I am. Then decide for yourself."

Unable to resist the temptation, he lowered his head to her neat curls and took a long lick.

Oh yeah, she was more than ready. Wet and moist and totally open to him, exactly as he had been fantasizing about for days now.

Samuel indulged himself a moment, licking and sucking at her damp, soft flesh. Chloe bucked her hips and moaned, enjoying his attentions. Each lick of her skin tasted like spicy honey, each buck of her hips drove him nearer to madness.

His boner would go down in personal history as the biggest, hardest hard-on he had ever experienced.

When he could stand it no longer and Chloe was tugging on his hair, he lifted himself up her body, laying soft, teasing kisses on her stomach.

"Was there something you wanted?" he teased.

He gasped and nearly came as she gently grabbed his cock in her hand. Resisting the urge to spend right there in her soft little hand, Samuel bit the inside of his cheek.

"Yeah," she huskily murmured, his brain hardly registering his words, "there is something you have that I want. Wanna share?"

Samuel grinned around his grimace. So she wanted to play rough, huh? He pulled her legs together, surprising her. Flipping her over, he laid her on her stomach and pushed her legs up so her ass rode high in the air.

"Uh…Sam…?"

Ignoring her, he then spread her legs, so she could feel the slight pull of muscles just at her entrance. Doggy style was one of his favorite positions, and with one's legs drawn right up, the muscles stretching, the pleasure was that much stronger.

"I'm always willing to share with you, little girl. Anything and everything I have."

With those heated words whispered in her ear, he thrust himself inside her to the hilt. She cried out, her position intensifying the pleasure. Grabbing her thighs, Samuel very slowly, very gently, pulled her legs back a fraction.

He wanted to stretch her hips and buttock muscles, but not enough to cause her pain. When her groans and screams reached a certain pitch he stopped, and let himself pulse inside her.

Her pussy clenched him like a tight fist, her inner walls milking him, urging him onto his own release. Samuel gritted his teeth, and slowly began to pull out.

"Oh no! No, no, no, no, no," Chloe muttered, barely lucid. When only his tip was lodged inside her, he held her hips and legs steady and plunged directly back in.

"*Yes!*" she screamed, nearly sobbing with the pleasure.

Over and over he plunged into her, in and out, in and out. Until finally her walls started contracting around him, squeezing his breath from his lungs.

Once more, he promised himself, let him hold on for Chloe one more time. Obviously his vixen had other ideas. As she came, she tightened her own muscles, causing the pressure on his cock to increase and his own control to snap.

Grabbing her hips much harder than he had intended, he held her in position and plunged inside her, erupting within two strokes.

Over and over he came, until he felt his seed trickling out her pussy and down his own thighs. He filled her, both physically and with his seed.

Exhausted, they both collapsed on the bed.

Chapter Seventeen

❧

Man, thought Chloe, *if that was fast and out of control, I can't wait till he really tries to fuck me hard and long.*

Stretching her legs she felt the age-old twinge of a well-fucked woman. Grinning, she looked up at Samuel. The color in his face was dying down, and neither of them was panting quite so hard anymore.

She let her eyes roll over his face. He was staring at the ceiling, seemingly in shock, so she let her gaze linger.

He was certainly handsome—all the Rutledge men were—but there was something extra that drew her to this particular brother. Chloe assumed it had nothing to do with him being the single one, but more to do with the electric feeling in the air when they shared the same space.

As she pondered this feeling and its possible ramifications, Samuel turned onto his side and looked at her. Gently, he began to caress her cheek.

"I'm sorry."

She blinked, wondering if she had only caught the second half of his comment.

"Sorry? Huh? About what?"

Samuel continued stroking her cheek. If he kept that up she'd jump him for real this time… *Hmmm*…she pondered.

"I meant to take you more slowly," he continued to stroke her cheek, moving up to her hairline where he started running his long fingers through her hair. "I meant to make this last longer."

Chloe rolled out from under his arm and sat on her knees. The bed was huge, she realized as she looked around. Ducking the hand he reached out, she knelt between his legs, nudging them wider apart.

She watched him grin and preen.

"Something on your mind, love?"

She grinned back. "Something," she agreed.

Bending down, she inhaled his musky scent. She could smell her own lighter scent on his skin, and in a strange way that pleased her. She could smell their sweat and commingled juices, all overlaid by Samuel's unique, masculine scent.

She bent her head in an imitation of what Samuel had previously done to her, and nuzzled his lightly furred balls. She saw him clench his fists next to her on the sheets, saw the slight arching of his back.

It amused her to see the power she held over him. Yet strangely at the same time it created a warm fuzzy feeling deep inside her chest. Firmly, she pushed *that* thought aside. No sense in going there.

Letting his soft hair rub over her nose and cheek, she inhaled him deeper into her system.

After a moment of enjoying this, she let her tongue trail oh-so-lightly around his soft skin, now slightly firmer, around his balls.

Licking them and toying with him with her tongue, she indulged herself for a moment, before quickly encasing him in her mouth. For just a moment, she enjoyed the strange sensation of sucking a man's balls. Never having done it before, it was strange, but fun at the same time.

After a minute of rolling the strange sac around her mouth, being careful to keep her teeth away from the delicate skin, she removed her mouth. A groan of disappointment slipped from Samuel's mouth, but before he could complain she quickly enveloped his half-erect cock in her mouth instead.

Warm and damp, she sucked tightly on him, creating exquisite pressure while gently sheathing her teeth. When

Samuel groaned, sounding as if he were about to die of pain, she loosened her suction slightly.

"No!" he cried out. "Don't stop! Please!"

Realizing it was a pleasurable pain, Chloe instantly returned her mouth's pressure, twice as hard. Bobbing her head slightly, and licking as much of the head as she could reach with her tongue, Chloe enjoyed the salty, manly taste of Samuel's pre-cum, mixed with their fluids from earlier. It was a strange taste, yet oddly pleasant.

As she felt Samuel harden to rock-like proportions, she felt some indescribable emotion well up inside her.

She had come here this weekend to work out what her heart's passion was, what her life passion could become. While teaching certainly fulfilled part of that passion, Chloe had the strange sensation that this also was a part of her destiny.

She felt such a connection to Samuel, had felt this connection since Mary's wedding where she had first met the man.

Sucking him and gently fisting his huge length in her much smaller hand gave her such a feeling of power, of satisfaction. She took him further into her mouth, determined to swallow as much of him as possible without making a fool of herself and gagging.

She smiled around his huge thickness as she decided to use the intimate knowledge of Samuel's fantasies to seduce him into a willing love slave. If she could fall head over ass in love with him, then the least he could do would be to return the favor.

Now, what was that fantasy he described? Ah yes, a wanton, beautiful woman astride him, taking her own pleasure from him, on top of him, and giving him immense pleasure in return.

Chloe snickered.

Piece of cake.

She grinned as her inner wanton unfurled and took over her mind.

Relaxing her throat muscles and inhaling deeply through her nose, Chloe took Samuel even deeper down her throat. Sucking tightly and letting her tongue caress the throbbing veins along his shaft, she mentally plotted her next move.

Let the games begin.

Chapter Eighteen

ဢ

Samuel closed his eyes and tried not to writhe in pleasure. Chloe had virtually swallowed his whole shaft—no mean feat—and the pleasure her tongue was giving him, not to mention the suction she wielded like a pro, was going to be the end of him. His balls were tight and fit to burst, and in about a nanosecond he would be shooting his seed down her throat.

Before he could reach that incredible peak, however, Chloe continued fisting his shaft, but removed her warm, wet, indescribable mouth.

"No..." he gasped, totally out of breath from the pleasure, "please don't! Chloe, don't leave me here!"

He, who prided himself on his control and skills between the sheets, was reduced to begging. If he wasn't so in love with the girl he might resent the power she wielded over him.

When he could breathe again, think coherently without desperately craving to drag her underneath him and fuck her raw, he intended to seduce her and keep her here with him—somehow. It was a problem for later.

"Patience, Samuel, I thought big-shot private eyes knew how to be patient."

Samuel choked on his laughter. "My dear, *no* man alive is patient when having his cock sucked so perfectly. Anyone who says differently is either bragging or an outright liar."

"Hmmm..." she murmured, her face lost in contemplation. Samuel stared at her, at the angles of her face, at the dark, soulful brown of her eyes, and the blonde highlights in her hair. While lost in the lust of his thoughts, he barely noticed Chloe sitting upright. When she began to stroke his shaft again, oh-so-lightly, he writhed in the pleasure.

"Do you remember what you said one of your favorite fantasies was?"

Samuel nodded his head, too caught up in the sensations to verbalize a response.

"I think it's only fair of me to make one of them come true for you. So hold on tight."

With that, she angled his cock just right, so she could impale herself on him. They both moaned, him in abject pleasure as his shaft was embraced in her tight, wet heat, her at the incredible hardness and pressure from the different angle.

She sat down fully on him, and he stared up at her. The warm lamplight made the blonde in her brown hair come out, cast a glow on her skin. He reached up and noticed his hands were shaking slightly. He palmed her breasts and enjoyed their smooth softness.

She sat up slightly, pulling away from him and replaced his hands with her own. Enchanted, he let his hands fall away and stared like a man possessed.

Slowly, she began to ride him, up and down, up and down, creating friction and the best sort of pleasure a man could hope to receive. She played with her breasts, tweaking the nipples already standing out for attention. Up and down, up and down she rode, driving him out of his mind.

Samuel felt the pressure begin to build yet again, but this time was determined she find her ultimate pleasure as well.

"It's better," he panted, "if you angle yourself like *this*."

And with that he held her hips just a moment and turned her slightly, so he could penetrate her deeper.

She cried out, her hands falling away from her breasts as she grabbed his waist for stability.

"Oh my, yes," she panted. "That is definitely a better angle. It's amazing how *deep* your knowledge of a woman's anatomy is."

Holding his waist for the new angle, she lifted herself and rushed back down onto his huge shaft. Moving faster now, not so intent on teasing anymore, she worked them both faster, sweat beginning to bead on her flushed skin.

"I can feel you so deeply, Samuel. This is incredible!"

"Move faster, Chloe. I'm burning up here."

Grunting and moaning, they both moved together in synch. The sound of flesh hitting flesh, their panting breaths, filled the small room, and Samuel worried he would explode before Chloe could find her own satisfaction.

Thankfully, when he began to think of taking control of their lovemaking, Chloe threw her head back and moaned from deep in her throat. He felt her walls contracting around him and he sat up to get as deeply as possible inside her. Put off-balance, she grabbed his back, holding onto him so she wouldn't fall.

In a single motion once her contractions eased, he laid her back and came down on top of her, thrusting himself the entire way up inside her. Finally able to release himself, he came in a single thrust. Yelling his release, he spent himself inside her, and collapsed, completely exhausted.

After a moment, Chloe wriggled and he turned onto his side. Gently, he stroked her sweat-slicked skin, enjoying the soft, satiny feel of her.

"That was fantastic. Thank you, Chloe-girl."

She smiled.

"You gotta stop stroking me," she mumbled, her eyes still closed. "I'm tired, I don't have your stamina. Let me nap a bit and wake me later."

Still stroking her, he kept his touch light to let her ease into sleep. He certainly would wake her later, but being a true gentleman, he let her sleep for now. After two rocketing orgasms, he could afford to let her sleep.

For half an hour or so.

Chapter Nineteen
Early Sunday Morning

ဢ

Chloe sat in the tiny café and sipped her cup of English Breakfast tea. Eyeing the full pot in front of her, she hoped she wouldn't burst if she drank the lot. Tea had a tendency to soothe her and help her think, something she needed a lot of right now. The only problem with drinking tea and thinking was as soon as one stopped drinking, one had to rush to the nearest restroom.

She looked outside the café windows at the weak sun trying to shine through the morning fog. She had a feeling the fog would burn off as the day wore on, and the thought of sitting out in the newly weeded garden in the sun made her feel a little lighter, but really her mind was on other things.

Last night had been so full-on, so intense she had felt the need to be alone for an hour or two this morning. It had seemed every time one or both of them had turned around they were caressing each other, Samuel would be suckling her nipples or she would be stroking his shaft.

She had no problem with their intense lovemaking—it was more she needed a breather, needed to clear her head. With Samuel thrusting inside her, or even laying calmly beside her in his huge bed, everything was jumbled. She couldn't possibly think straight.

And so she had pleaded exhaustion—which was truth—and decided to take a drive. She hadn't gone with any direction or intention, she just needed some air. She had ended up back in the small village she recalled passing on her way to Mary and Dominic's cabin.

A few small shops and a scattered bunch of houses made up the small village. She remembered wishing she could stop at the café for a bite to eat on first passing through, but it had been closed at the late hour she passed.

Now seemed the perfect time to pop in and drink a cup of tea and contemplate the world.

Sighing, she took another sip, wondering where the waitress had gone off to. It was admittedly quite early in the morning, but looking around the shop, Chloe realized it was just she and a very old looking woman sitting over in the other corner of the shop. No one else could be seen.

As her eyes fell on the old woman she lifted a hand and waved Chloe over to her. Mentally shrugging, she picked up her cup and the pot of tea and headed over. Even though she really wanted to think her situation through, conversely she didn't really feel like being alone.

Chloe grinned. Sometimes she just couldn't be pleased.

Setting the pot down in the middle of the old lady's table, Chloe gently put her cup down and sat opposite the lady. Noticing the other diner's empty cup, she offered, "Would you like a nice hot cup of English Breakfast, ma'am? I have a pot here."

The old crone smiled happily. Her eyes were the very palest blue Chloe had ever seen, and very slightly cloudy. The sparkle inside them, however, was sharp.

"I would love a cup, dear. That silly young chit has gone out back to *talk* to her lover, so it will be a while before she gets back."

Chloe happily poured the other woman a cup of tea, grateful to be sharing the huge pot.

"I'm so glad, I was wondering how I would drink the lot of it. I'm Chloe by the way — Mary Rutledge's cousin."

"I know who you are, dear. I'm Old Mona. Been around these parts forever. You're that rascal Samuel's mate, aren't you?"

Chloe blinked, not knowing what to say and still be polite. Taking a sip of tea instead, she pondered her responses. Old Mona seemed like such a nice old woman, she didn't want to upset her by trying to explain the more modern concept of taking a lover.

"Umm...I'm more of a casual acquaintance actually."

Mona waved her hand as if to cast the lie from the air.

"Oh posh! You're not merely lovers. Women have been taking on lovers for centuries, my dear. There's nothing new in that. But finding a mate, now *that* is a rarer occasion. Particularly finding one's True Mate, one's heart's passion. That takes a mixture of patience, determination, and pure luck."

Chloe felt a niggling worry at the term "True Mate" and "Heart's Passion". It was well and good to realize she finally had found a heartfelt passion for teaching, and wanted to truly make her career out of it. But to associate such strong terms to a man who had easily had over a hundred lovers in his life, and had never felt the need to commit to any of them, that was a lot scarier.

Almost as if she had read her mind, Mona put down her cup of tea and leaned forward. Chloe had the distinct impression the old woman wished to shake her like a silly five-year-old.

"Don't be crazy, my dear. Men have always played the field, or 'sowed their wild oats' as we called it in my day. Once they find The One, they settle down and become respectable men, or a whole lot more respectable than the rogues they were. All those Rutledge boys have turned out beautifully, even if they were hellions as children and teenagers. Everyone despaired of them when they caroused well into their late twenties and in Dom and Samuel's case—early thirties."

The old lady shook her head, but Chloe noticed a twinkle in her eye.

"Only their Grandpa Zach and I didn't worry about them. Those boys had been through enough—they deserved their time. And both he and I remembered well how one's True Mate merely pops up when one least expects it. You can't force something like that. We knew that sooner or later those boys would meet their match, and who were we to try and force them down a path they didn't want?"

Chloe frowned, only understanding a bit of the conversation, and not having a clue where it was leading.

"And so, young lady, you have some decisions to make."

"Me?" she queried.

Mona rolled her eyes, not unlike how Mary often did when she was being most dense.

"No, the ghostly spirit over there in the corner. Of course you, girl!" With the way this conversation was going, Chloe turned around to look behind her, half expecting some ghostly specter to be fluttering in the corner. Thankfully for her sanity, nothing was there.

"Well," she started, feeling strangely safe talking to this woman, "I had expected to take some time out up here. I needed to find a passion for something in my work. I've been casting about for years now, just flitting from one job to the other. None of them really touched me, deep in here," she rested one hand over her chest, near her heart.

Feeling a bit silly, she picked up her cup and sipped her tea again. Realizing the cup was empty, she poured another, refilling Mona's at the same time.

Carefully replacing the half-empty pot, she lifted the thin china to her lips and took a sip.

"While weeding yesterday, I finally hit upon teaching. I subbed for a friend last semester, and really liked it, but I think I'd prefer the younger kids. Get them to love learning and teach them how to deal with life and all it throws at you. I really think it could be a passion, but at the same time I'm not sure if I should go back to college to get the diploma."

Mona nodded as she drank her tea, patiently waiting for her to work through her thoughts.

Chloe squirmed, instinctively knowing what Mona was waiting for.

"I feel very deeply for Samuel... Umm...he's a great guy...but...umm..."

Mona put her cup down and rolled her eyes.

"Oh for goodness sake, girl! The youth of today! He won't bite you, not unless you ask nicely. He's an upstanding, decent man. He's certainly half in love with you, and quite possibly pacing his floor as we speak trying to convince himself to take a risk on you. It's a bit different for us wolves. We feel the mateship bond a lot more intensely than you humans do. We can't just put it off or talk ourselves out of it."

Obviously picking up on how rattled Chloe was becoming, the old lady sat back and picked up her tea again. Sipping it thoughtfully, she started again.

"How about we make a deal? You think about whether you can take a chance on the boy, and give him a chance when he talks to you?"

Chloe chuckled and drank the last of her tea. "Are you considered the town's matchmaker?"

Mona chuckled, obviously picking up the teasing quality in her voice.

"Not at all child, I'm considered the Pack's interfering old lady. I don't limit myself merely to matchmaking. I interfere in every aspect of their lives. I grouch when they don't eat properly, when they carouse and make fools of themselves, and when the young ones don't treat their passing fancies right."

Chloe laughed outright. Pouring the remaining tea into their now empty cups, she replaced the pot and sat back.

"I bet the Rutledge men just *loved you*!"

The old lady chuckled, the gleam in her eye more pronounced.

"Those young lads *still* cringe and stand taller when they see me coming. They fix their jeans when they're with their mates and inevitably hold their babies so I can't demand a hello kiss. They're a big bunch of babies. Their wives are good girls though, your Mary included. They spoil me rotten, and the babies are gorgeous."

Chloe smiled and was going to ask a few questions, when Mona put her cup down.

"Well, I'd best be off back home. Tom and Zach will be dropping by soon to make sure my cupboards aren't bare. Silly things, as if I'd ever starve!"

Chloe helped the old lady stand, anxiously fluttering around her.

"Are you sure you don't want a lift home, or I could do some shopping for you, if you'd prefer?"

"Posh, don't be silly girl. You go back and think over what I've said. There's a lot there you need to go over, and a lot you need to organize before your cousin comes back tomorrow, hmm?"

Chloe smiled and wondered where Mona had heard when Mary was coming home. Mona turned around after a few steps.

"Oh, I nearly forgot. The reason I asked you over was to tell you the local town, back down that track a ways, is looking for an elementary teacher. Nothing full-time. The local school closed down years ago—so all the kids head off into the city to learn. As there's so many from around these woodland parts, they try to keep the teachers of the babies local. It was just a thought, but I think you'd have made it on your own. Just wanted to let you know."

With that the old woman exited the café and hobbled across the street. Chloe sat back down and stared at the empty cups. The local school was looking for a new teacher?

She hadn't thought to inquire around the local area; she hadn't thought she would be staying. Now she had a head full of questions and no idea where to start.

The waitress chose that moment to come back into the café, rather rumpled and her bun askew. Looking faintly flushed and very satisfied, she headed over.

"Oh, I'm glad you shared your tea with Old Mona, she doesn't get out much and really enjoys talking people's ears off. I hope she didn't freak you out, she's a little weird."

Chloe smiled a bit frostily, feeling very protective of the old woman.

"Not at all, she's the sanest person I've spoken to in months."

Handing over a few bills and some change, she stood up. The waitress looked a bit embarrassed.

"I just meant she sometimes weirds out the outsiders."

"Ah, but I'm not exactly an outsider. I'm a cousin of the Rutledges."

Suddenly the waitress was looking her over carefully.

"You're house-sitting for Mary and Dom, aren't you?" she nodded as if confirming something in her own mind. "That explains it."

Losing the thread of the conversation, once again, Chloe smiled and figured it was way beyond time to finish her shopping and head back. She had a special dinner to prepare and a seduction to plan.

Saying goodbye to the waitress, she headed over to the small grocery store, hoping to score a few deals for the dinner she had planned.

Chapter Twenty

ဆ

Chloe lifted the Dutch oven's lid and gave one last stir to her beef goulash. She was expecting Samuel to arrive any minute now and she wanted everything to be ready before they started tonight. As she dipped her knife into the large pot, she felt that womanly pride as the beef fell apart at the slight touch. It was cooked to perfection. The potatoes were soft and just fine. She turned the heat down to a low simmer and placed the knife in the sink to be washed.

Pleased with herself and the way her meal turned out, Chloe turned around to open the fridge door. There was a knock at the front door just as she was lifting the large bowl of tossed salad out of the fridge.

"I'll be there in a second!" she called out. Placing the bowl on the counter, she wiped her hands on a towel and crossed over to the door. As she swung it open she saw Samuel on her front porch, sniffing the air appreciatively.

"Ever thought to be a cook?" he greeted her. She stepped back and smiled.

"Nope. I couldn't bear to work in a boiling hot kitchen day in, day out. That and it's too cutthroat working your way up. Far too many secrets, and tempers, and jealousy in a kitchen. You know the saying—too many cooks and all that."

"Mmm...I brought the game."

Chloe waved a hand to the small coffee table. "Just leave it there, I figured you'd want to eat first. I cooked up a huge amount, I know you so well."

She was startled when he bent over her, carefully holding her chin still so he could lean down to kiss her. The tenderness she felt in the kiss, the gentle, almost sweet exploration of her mouth had her flush with surprise.

This wasn't a simple hey-there-good-to-see-you sort of kiss. No. This was more of a missed-you-like-crazy-why-did-you-take-so-long style of kiss. An affirmation of the night they had spent together as well as an indication of more to come.

Chloe felt quite dazed as he pulled away. Blinking, she tried to gather her thoughts. She had planned to feed the man, make sure he was comfortable and then tell him her plan to talk to the local school principal and submit a request to teach in the local school. As their relationship was barely a weekend old, she hadn't thought it much of his business whether she left or stayed.

That kiss, however, showed her he was more than interested in what her plans were, as well as his intention to stay in her life. She had had every intention of continuing their relationship—but it seemed as if he was moving a little faster than she had anticipated.

She had thought of maybe renting a cabin in the region somewhere, dating the man for a few months. Having a normal, ordinary courtship to see if they worked well together.

What was it Mona had said?

Ah, yes. *"We feel the mateship bond a lot more intensely than you humans do. We can't just put it off or talk ourselves out of it."*

For a split second, Chloe worried that Samuel was moving too fast. She was brought back to reality, however, when he pulled her ponytail gently.

"Hey there, little girl! Don't freak on me, it was just a kiss."

Chloe laughed and shook her head. She was being silly. "Go and sit down before my goulash burns. I'd never forgive you for that. It would be so embarrassing."

Samuel grinned cheekily. "Hey, it wasn't me staring off into space, looking ready to bolt, and chewing on my lower lip."

Chloe shrugged off his teasing and went to serve the dinner.

* * * * *

When Samuel finally rested his fork on his plate and sat back with a satisfied sigh, Chloe breathed a sigh of relief. For a moment there she had worried he would want fourths, and while there was a small amount of the goulash left, there wasn't enough to *fill* his plate a fourth time. He had inhaled his huge first serving, automatically checking if she wanted seconds and heading back into the kitchen to replenish his plate.

After a second serving of both the goulash and salad, mopping up the remaining gravy with the last crust of the French roll she had bought them, he had held up his plate in an imitation of Oliver Twist.

"Please, miss. I would greatly appreciate some more."

Chloe had taken in her own empty dish, leaving it to soak in the sink, and heaped his plate a third time. Thinking to teach him a lesson, she had filled the plate, as full as she had the first time, nearly — but not quite — emptying the large pot.

Seeing his eyes light up as she placed the plate in front of him, she had marveled how such a lithe, slim man could pack away such a vast quantity of food.

She had debated for a moment if she should warn him of the ice cream and cream puffs she had picked up for dessert, but as she wouldn't be able to squeeze a bite more in, she figured to leave it for later.

They had talked politely over dinner. She had explained about her previous careers, how nothing had really grabbed and held her attention until she had found teaching. But far more interestingly, Samuel had opened up about his work as a private investigator.

She found it so interesting, the security work he did with his brothers, how in the beginning when he had been building his reputation and starting out, he had followed around cheating spouses and proving false claims.

He insisted much of it was incredibly boring—paperwork, research, and very little action. But she was still entranced by the work. He had laughed when she divulged she had learned to pick locks from a former boyfriend back in high school.

"Finally full?" she teased as she grinned at him.

He patted his totally flat stomach. "Gotta keep my energy up. You certainly wouldn't want me to falter and run out of energy at a critical time, would you?"

Chloe laughed as she picked up his plate. "No. I certainly wouldn't want you to deflate at the wrong moment."

Chuckling, she rinsed his plate and placed it in the sink to soak with the other dishes.

Walking back into the main room, she was surprised to find him already sitting on the couch, arm spread out, inviting her to sit right beside him.

"Eager tonight, are you?" she laughed.

"Come on, we have stuff to do. Don't want to waste all that warmth and energy that delicious meal gave me."

Laughing, she sat next to him and relaxed into his warm chest. When his arm gently curved around her, she felt as if she had finally come home.

"You mentioned how much you enjoyed teaching. Are you going to continue it, even though your subbing is finished?"

She leaned back to look up to him.

"I met this really wonderful old woman at the café today. Mona. She said there was a need for an elementary teacher in the local school back in the main town. It's a fairly short distance from here, only about an hour. I might rent an apartment in the city, or maybe a cabin halfway between here and the town, so I can be closer to Mary. Matthew is already in town, and will be heading back off to college again soon."

She shrugged. "I'm not sure they'll even hire me, but I really think I'd enjoy it. I think I've finally found where my passion lies."

Samuel started nuzzling her neck. She giggled as he growled and gently nipped her neck.

"Surely not *all* your passion is in teaching kids?"

Giggling, she wriggled, trying to escape out of his arms. He tightened his hold and continued nipping her neck, insisting on a response.

"Well, I seem to have a lot of other passion for one long, thick, warm object. But at the moment the teaching is looking really promising."

Laughing outright as he growled and rolled them both onto the floor, she wriggled as he trapped her body underneath his own much larger one.

"Only teaching is looking promising, huh? What do you say we go back to playing Dominic's card game?"

Without lessening the pressure on her, he lifted one arm up, felt around until he held the small box of cards, and pulled off the lid.

Only a single card was inside the box. It had a red border, with "Advanced: for those who *dare*" emblazoned on it.

Chloe sobered up, her laughter dying away. She had a funny feeling about this.

Samuel sat up, sitting on his knees on the floor and offered her the box, looking incongruous with its solitary card inside.

Chloe reached out to take the card, idly noticing her hand shook very faintly as she reached for the card. Picking it out, she turned it over.

I love you. You are my heart's passion, Chloe. Marry me. Please.

The script was not the typed print of the other cards. Obviously the game had come with a number of red-rimmed cards that were blank, for the man or woman to fill in themselves.

The bold, masculine script could only be Samuel's.

Chloe looked up to the man who sat opposite her. Opening her mouth, she tried to form words. Nothing would come. She was so totally shocked.

Samuel stared at her, his beautiful blue eyes piercing her with his intensity.

"It's simple, Chloe. I love you. I think I fell in love with you at Dom and Mary's wedding. I just didn't want to admit that such a young, willowy woman could bring me to my knees. I want to help you reach your dreams, want you to realize all your passions, particularly those of your heart. But most of all, I want to be your heart's passion."

Chloe felt a tear trickle down her face. Sitting up she threw her arms around Samuel.

"Oh my, that was the most beautiful proposal. You *are* my heart's passion, Samuel. Your fantasies make me so hot I want to bring each and every one true. I want to come home from school to see your smiling, cheeky face. Yes. I'll marry you."

With a groan, he swept her close for a soul-searing kiss. Plucking the card from her hand, he let it drop to the floor and rolled them over so she was astride him.

"Ride me, baby," he groaned. "Ride me until we both burst."

Eagerly, they stripped each other until they were both naked. Chloe pumped his cock with her hand, once, then twice. As a tiny pearl of pre-cum squeezed out of his tip, she murmured and bent down to lick it up. Rolling it around in her mouth, she reached up and kissed him firmly on his mouth, letting him taste their mingled essence.

"Please, baby," he groaned, tilting his hips suggestively at her.

Grinning, she teased his nipple.

"Patience," she intoned.

"Fuck patience," he muttered, bending his head to take her nipple in his mouth. She gasped at the shock that ran through her body. She felt the world moving, and realized it was only Samuel rolling her underneath him, pushing aside the coffee table with a loud *thunk*, so they didn't hit their heads at a busy moment. Laughing, she caressed his shaft and balls.

"What happened to me riding you?"

"Next time," he promised.

With one, fierce thrust, he was inside her, both of them moaning in pleasure. Chloe stroked the delicate skin between his shaft and balls, and he lightly fingered her clit. She was amazed at how quickly she felt herself spinning out of control. Before she could even catch her breath she felt her head arch back into the rug, her back bow out and the climax tear through her.

A split second later, Samuel was shouting, thrusting even deeper inside her, his seed erupting deep inside her.

He collapsed on top of her and they panted, catching their breaths. Chloe resolved to turn him over as soon as her lethargic muscles would move.

The air was pierced by the shrill ringing of the phone. Chloe frowned.

What the hell?

She looked at Samuel, who shrugged.

"No one knows I'm here. It's not for me."

"But no one knows I'm here either."

Lifting himself up on one arm, cursing at the coffee table, Samuel looked around until he saw the phone on a small table by the window. Getting up, uncaring of his nudity, he picked it up.

"Hello?"

Chloe could hear a feminine voice on the other end. She sat up, wondering who on earth it could be. Before she could wonder and begin to panic, Samuel laughed out loud.

"Really? What were the two of you doing this time?"

More talking from the other voice.

"Ahh...I understand. Yeah, she's here, hang on."

Samuel crossed back over to her, taking the cordless phone with him. He sat back down on the soft carpet and handed her the phone. He mouthed the word, "Mary". Understanding dawned, and then embarrassment set in.

"Uh...hi, Mar. How's the dirty weekend going?"

"Pathetically. Never make love out in the rain. It's romantic, but messy as hell and now Dominic has a bad cold. We're coming back tonight. I take it you've had an interesting weekend yourself?"

Pretending to misunderstand, Chloe agreed.

"Oh yes. I've decided to do elementary teaching. There's an opening back in town. It's not that far from you, and Matthew is back there after all."

Mary laughed. "Fine. Be that way. Can you spend the night at Samuel's?"

Chloe looked over at him, and drew a quick breath as he started sucking her nipple again, waggling his eyebrows in a comical manner.

"Umm...probably. I think we're going to get married a little later."

Mary laughed.

"Just wait until I tell Dom. He owes me twenty bucks now."

Chloe frowned.

"Huh?"

"We knew something was up at the wedding. I said it was love, Dominic insisted it was lust and Samuel would forget it. I gave you both ten months to work it out, so I win the money. I'll split it with you. If you get married within six months, I get a further fifty."

Chloe laughed.

"I'll think about it. We haven't set a date yet, but it's a pretty safe bet to be within six months. You owe me a night on the town, maybe something new and exotic for the Hen's Night."

Samuel jerked his head back and frowned menacingly, waggling his finger in a comical manner. Just to tease him, Chloe continued over Mary's voice.

"Maybe we can call in a few favors. I hear there are some fantastic strippers in town. We can work out the details later."

As Samuel reached out to grab the phone, she laughed again. "Gotta run, see you tomorrow."

Pressing the end button, she hung up as Mary protested.

Grinning hugely, she explained to Samuel.

"Your brother bet Mary that it was just lust between us. She bet him twenty bucks we'd be together within ten months, and an extra fifty bucks that we'd be married six months after that. Surely you can't blame me for their deal?"

"No," he growled as he rolled onto his back and pulled her on top of him, "but you're not to go to a bar, and you certainly aren't going to see any damned exotic stripper. You realize we're the only ones who haven't met in a bar? I don't want to tempt fate. Anyway, if you want to see a stripper I'll be happy to oblige you."

Chloe smiled and bent down to kiss him. She had months to talk him around if she chose to.

"You're my passion, Samuel. There's no need to worry. We can work it out later. Right now, there's a certain fantasy I recall you mentioning. Something about a woman pleasuring herself as well as her partner…"

"Mmm," he agreed, "later sounds good. So does that fantasy, but right now I have a much deeper need to be inside you, not being teased out of my mind."

Chloe smiled, letting him have his way *this* time. She didn't protest when Samuel lay her down on the soft rug, covering her body with his own. He dipped his head to her pussy, kissing her in the most intimate way a man can, and then raised himself to cover her again.

Kissing her mouth this time, he shared their mingled tastes with her. Chloe enjoyed the tangy yet sweet taste of them joined. It soothed her. She arched as his wicked hands began stroking her. Her sides, teasingly over her breasts, he warmed her with his intimate, knowing touch.

When he moved his head down to the juncture between her neck and shoulder, she moaned. Like most women, she was particularly sensitive around there.

She felt shocked when she felt a tiny sting of sharp teeth, then a soothing, warm laving of his tongue. She felt…filled by Samuel, but not in a sexual sense. It was as if he had left a part of himself in the small bite.

"What…?"

Samuel lifted his hand to her ear. "I marked you, love, mingled our essences and souls. We belong to each other."

Raising an eyebrow, not sure if he was being poetic or dead serious, Chloe decided to let it ride for now. There was something much *harder* that she wanted.

Deciding enough foreplay had occurred, they could always take it slowly next time, she assured herself, she gently took a hold of his cock. Lightly teasing him, running her slightly cold hands up and down the hot shaft, she snickered at his hastily indrawn breath.

"You don't want to get me started too quickly, baby," he warned.

"Wanna bet?" she teased.

"Fine, don't blame me then," he replied, turning her over onto her hands and knees. Chloe arched her back so she wiggled her ass at him. She was dripping and more than ready for playtime to begin.

With no more caresses, no preliminaries, Samuel thrust balls deep inside her. Chloe arched even more, cried out, and without thought closed her eyes. The pleasure radiated out from her and she couldn't believe how intensely she felt Samuel filling her from this position. Just his first simple thrust had her feeling the beginnings of her orgasm just out of reach.

It started in the pit of her stomach, the growing, electric feelings of the wave of satisfaction. It hovered just a moment out of reach, until Samuel withdrew himself slightly, and then plunged back in.

Chloe felt shocked, surprised really, as his second thrust was enough to push her over. She tightened her muscles, squeezed her ass and stomach, and made her insides squeeze his cock.

She assumed it worked as Samuel let out a low, almost painful-sounding groan and held her hips tightly as he plunged deeper inside her, erupting and filling her with his seed.

They collapsed together on the rug, panting and sweating. Samuel pulled her close, spooning her and holding her tightly.

"We need to get a ring," he said panting.

Chloe simply nodded, still trying to stop her head from spinning from the intensity of the climax.

"We need to get you that teaching job and signed up for classes for your diploma, as well."

Chloe smiled sleepily, glad Samuel took such an interest in her and listened to what she talked to him about.

Chloe closed her eyes, thinking wistfully of a warm bath and nap in a warm bed. Before she could begin to fall asleep, however, there was a strange buzzing noise coming from the dinner table.

"Shit," Samuel complained, "who the hell...?"

Regretting the loss of his warm body, Chloe snuggled deeper into the rug, determined to catch the nap she had thought about.

"We need to get the hell out of here."

Chloe opened one eye at Samuel's words. "Mmm?" she inquired.

"That was Dominic IMing me. ETA 10 minutes, he says. Which means we have to get dressed and clean the signs of debauchery. Maybe even put the cooking pans to soak."

Chloe blinked again and reluctantly pulled herself into a sitting position.

"How about you put the stuff to soaking while I grab a quick shower?" At the sparkle and mischievous look in his eyes, she hastily added, "Alone! Just think of how shocked Dominic would be to find us making out in his shower. He'd never let us live it down."

Chloe smiled as Samuel pouted, but obediently moved into the kitchen, pulling his jeans back on as he went.

Chloe gathered her clothes and headed into the bathroom, throwing things in her suitcase as she went. Peering at the small bite mark on her neck in the mirror, she smiled. It wasn't exactly how she had planned her time away, but somehow everything managed to be cruising along just fine.

Life was odd sometimes.

Good, but odd how things always managed to turn out well.

Smiling, she jumped into the shower. She needed to be at her best when Mary came in with that smug, "I told you so" attitude.

Epilogue

ഌ

Zachariah Rutledge stared deep into the flames of his fireplace. Shifting slightly on his cushion, he cursed his old bones and worn-out flesh.

He couldn't pass on just yet. The pieces were all in place. He had done his best. Roland and Helene were happy and secure. Roland had finally healed, forgiven his past, and embraced his future. Zachariah had redeemed that small piece of his own soul from his past mistake.

Yet, it was the mental picture of Edward who grabbed his attention deep in the flames. Young Edward. Even had he not been born when Roland returned, Zachariah would still have healed the man, still have repented the mistake he had unwittingly made with Roland's father and mother.

However, upon first seeing the child Edward, still a mere infant back then, he had known the boy's future and the future of Zachariah's own kin were intertwined. Zachariah knew he had what they used to call The Sight. All of his grandsons had it to some degree or other, yet he had it strongest. It was a knowing, an intuition. All he knew was that the very first time he laid eyes on young Edward he had known his future was tied with that of his kin.

And so his desire to help out the floundering family became even stronger.

He only hoped he had done what was right—what was good. He had always striven for that, for the best. Yet often one's intentions were not enough. In this instance, he hoped it was.

When baby Christiana had been born and presented to him, he had again intuitively known she was tied up in all this somehow. A part of him suspected both she and Edward were linked spiritually, souls as well as destinies. Yet, it wasn't for him to meddle. He had repaid his debt to Roland, and in turn young Edward. He refused to tamper with Fate and Destiny any more than he might have already done.

He shifted his body, uncomfortable even on the cushions and in front of the fire. He was just too damn old.

He had done his best, had set the pieces all up, nurtured them as best he could. He had been alone for so long. He could still feel his beloved Naomi beside him, calming him, supporting him. He knew he would be returning to her soon. With luck, his best would be enough this time around.

Zachariah closed his eyes, his meditation finishing. He let his favorite fantasy wash over him. His luscious Naomi, all soft curves and big smiles—forever loving him; holding him, embracing him. Even at his well-advanced age, he still lusted for her, loved her. Such was the bond of a mated werewolf pair. No other woman came even close for him. No other women, human or wolf, would ever be a tiny speck on his beloved wife.

He indulged himself in the fantasy, felt again her soft curves embracing him, felt her heated kisses along his neck. Felt her desire and love consume him in the best kind of flame. The flame of eternal love.

Yes. He would be joining his lost love very soon.

Why an electronic book?

We live in the Information Age—an exciting time in the history of human civilization, in which technology rules supreme and continues to progress in leaps and bounds every minute of every day. For a multitude of reasons, more and more avid literary fans are opting to purchase e-books instead of paper books. The question from those not yet initiated into the world of electronic reading is simply: *Why?*

1. ***Price.*** An electronic title at Ellora's Cave Publishing and Cerridwen Press runs anywhere from 40% to 75% less than the cover price of the exact same title in paperback format. Why? Basic mathematics and cost. It is less expensive to publish an e-book (no paper and printing, no warehousing and shipping) than it is to publish a paperback, so the savings are passed along to the consumer.

2. ***Space.*** Running out of room in your house for your books? That is one worry you will never have with electronic books. For a low one-time cost, you can purchase a handheld device specifically designed for e-reading. Many e-readers have large, convenient screens for viewing. Better yet, hundreds of titles can be stored within your new library—on a single microchip. There are a variety of e-readers from different manufacturers. You can also read e-books on your PC or laptop computer. (Please note that Ellora's Cave does not endorse any specific brands.

You can check our websites at www.ellorascave.com or www.cerridwenpress.com for information we make available to new consumers.)

3. *Mobility.* Because your new e-library consists of only a microchip within a small, easily transportable e-reader, your entire cache of books can be taken with you wherever you go.

4. *Personal Viewing Preferences.* Are the words you are currently reading too small? Too large? Too… ANNOYING? Paperback books cannot be modified according to personal preferences, but e-books can.

5. *Instant Gratification.* Is it the middle of the night and all the bookstores near you are closed? Are you tired of waiting days, sometimes weeks, for bookstores to ship the novels you bought? Ellora's Cave Publishing sells instantaneous downloads twenty-four hours a day, seven days a week, every day of the year. Our webstore is never closed. Our e-book delivery system is 100% automated, meaning your order is filled as soon as you pay for it.

Those are a few of the top reasons why electronic books are replacing paperbacks for many avid readers.

As always, Ellora's Cave and Cerridwen Press welcome your questions and comments. We invite you to email us at Comments@ellorascave.com or write to us directly at Ellora's Cave Publishing Inc., 1056 Home Avenue, Akron, OH 44310-3502.

Cerridwen, the Celtic Goddess of wisdom, was the muse who brought inspiration to storytellers and those in the creative arts. Cerridwen Press encompasses the best and most innovative stories in all genres of today's fiction. Visit our site and discover the newest titles by talented authors who still get inspired - much like the ancient storytellers did, once upon a time.

Cerridwen Press

www.cerridwenpress.com